Just One Kiss

Susanne Bellamy

ISBN 978-0-6484569-2-6

DEDICATION

Thanks to the men and women of the RFDS, medical, aeronautical, and support staff who do so much for distant and remote populations in our country.

This is for the two doctors in my family, my father-in-law, Dr Eryl Rees, and his granddaughter, Dr Eliza Wziontek.

Chapter One

"The horses are at the barrier . . . and they're off and racing in the Cloncurry Stakes. Big Mike takes an early lead but the favourite, Jester, is . . .." The race caller's excited voice blurred amid cheers from the crowd thronging the remote north-west Queensland racecourse.

Dr Dan Middleton glanced at the red dirt track and the dust cloud lazily settling over the race day crowd. Women dressed as smartly as those at Flemington on Cup Day teetered on high heels on hard-packed earth. If there were a few more plastic cups of beer than flutes of champagne, the effect was much the same.

He swallowed the last of his beer and swatted at the flies hovering near his mouth. Horses thundered around the final bend and the crowd surged towards the barriers. A whirly-wind picked up dust, swirling and tracking behind a slim, young woman, the only other racegoer not focused on the race. Caught unawares by the sudden gust, she turned her back and struggled to hold her hat and dress as it lifted in the wind. Her pink dress ballooned and flipped up like one of his mother's fuschias. Tanned legs went all the way up to a pair of silky white panties and Dan grinned.

As suddenly as it had risen, the wind dropped. The woman exhaled and swatted dust from her full skirt. Twitching the outfit into place, she continued towards the beer tent. And Dan.

Faint pink flared in her cheeks as her gaze connected with his and he realised he was still ogling her and grinning.

"Perv." She pushed past him, knocking the plastic cup out of his hand.

By the time he retrieved it and stood, she had disappeared into the crowd around the bar.

"Great way to make an impression, doc." Mike Maguire, a mechanic with the Royal Flying Doctor Service in Mt. Isa, raised his plastic cup of beer in a mock salute.

"Bad timing. Story of my life." How could he have let himself forget the perils of showing his appreciation of the female form? Surely he'd learned that lesson by now?

"How so, doc? Thought you'd have nurses hanging off your arm. Besides, our Amy's a pretty girl and—"

"Drop it, Mike. Not interested." Dan couldn't afford to be. As much as his job with the Royal Flying Doctor Service let him follow his passion for rural medicine, like his mother and grandfather before him, it was an opportunity to get away from the mud slinging. Although he was pleased his staff at Gosford Hospital had told the truth and stood up for him. And now—

"Don't say that too loud. People might think you're —"

"Gay?" he finished off for the burly mechanic.

"So you're not interested in Amy? She'll be relieved to hear that."

"I'm here to work. That's all. Why?"

"You're rostered on together. She's your pilot."

Amy Alistair peered into the small mirror in the ladies loo. Dust caked her face and her cleavage itched, and her new dress had acquired an unflattering layer of red that even the drycleaner would struggle to remove.

And her last-in-the-field horse was probably still running, which was why she'd been heading to the beer tent when the willy-willy sent her skirt flying and Mr Smug and Brooding had copped an eyeful.

Along with half the male population of town.

He'd been the first male she encountered after the wind caught her unawares, and maybe she'd overreacted but his amusement had ratcheted up her embarrassment and her temper had run away with her. Dull red had stained his cheeks as he bent to pick up the cup she'd knocked out of his hand.

She almost felt sorry for him. Until Mechanic Mark nudged him and nodded in her direction. Slinking behind two burly blokes propping up the bar, she sought a safe, non-windy corner where she could quietly sink into the floor. Thank goodness she'd be back in the Isa tomorrow and could get back into work trousers.

Sharyn, her nemesis at high school and all-round stuck-up prig since she'd won Miss North West Queensland, popped her head around the entrance and chuckled. "Hey, Amy, nice knickers. Didn't realise you were so hard up for a date that you'd flash everyone. But hey, you got the eye of the new hottie." With a snort, Sharyn waved her mobile phone and withdrew.

Damn the two-second rule. If Sharyn had seen Amy's awkward moment, the whole region would know by—Amy checked her watch—now.

Oh, hell, had Sharyn got photos too?

##

Amy cruised along the strip of highway back to The Isa, her iPod on shuffle. As her red ute crested a slight rise, the headlights caught on metallic silver paint and flashing hazard lights. She eased back on the accelerator and pulled in behind a car with its bonnet raised. Someone had left the races earlier than her, it seemed. And by the large dent in the bonnet, they'd encountered a roo on the highway back to Mt. Isa.

She switched her lights to low beam and stepped out of her ute. The driver appeared around the front of the car, holding a torch in one hand and shading his eyes with the other.

"Well, if that doesn't put the icing on this day." She bit her lip, hoping her muttered comment hadn't carried to the man.

"Thanks for stopping. I've lost a headlight and—" Mr Smug and Brooding stopped as she walked past the front of her car. Of course it had to be him broken down at the side of the road. She contemplated jumping back in her ute and hightailing it. For all of five seconds.

"Yeah, well, let's see how bad the damage is." Even to her own ears, her voice sounded snarky. But dammit, she'd bought a new dress and that stupid hat and even crammed her feet into high heels for the racing carnival in celebration of her promotion.

Stupid choice. When did any male look at Amy Alistair with more than friendship on his mind? She was one of the boys, not tall and elegant like Sharyn.

She held out her hand for his torch, stalked around to the front of his car and peered under the hood. With an ease born of familiarity with machinery on the family property, she assessed the damage. "Your radiator's taken a beating as well as the bonnet. I doubt it will get you to Mt. Isa tonight. You do know you can't drive over eighty on these roads after dusk?"

"I doubt I was doing even that. The roo was going faster than me." Annoyance tinged his voice and he shoved his hands into his pockets. "Any chance I can catch a lift with you?"

The last thing Amy wanted was this prig invading her space. But leaving him by the side of the road waiting for another ride wasn't an option. She wouldn't leave her worst enemy in such a fix, and he was far from that. Even if he had smirked at her wardrobe malfunction. She shuddered as she imagined the phrase with Sharyn's intonation. "Hop in."

"Thank you." Stiff formality crackled in those two words.

Amy sniffed and thumbed the torch off. Let him be in a snit. Maybe he wouldn't want to talk as they drove, and that would suit her fine.

Dan reached into the boot for his medical bag. He needed travelling with the belligerent blonde like he needed a hole in the head. Petite and feisty, she clearly didn't want his company. Maybe Amy had been given the lowdown on him already. If his reason for leaving Gosford had been leaked to his new employer, he could hardly begin with a clean slate. The thought depressed him before he remembered her obvious embarrassment at the races.

A memory of white silk and tanned thighs rushed back as he thought of their unfortunate meeting, and he slammed the boot. Thank God she didn't realise how clearly her ute's lights had outlined her curves as she'd approached him. High heels had been replaced by a pair of unlaced work boots but headlights through her filmy skirt revealed far more than swirling wind. Better not share that titbit or she'd order him out of her car. Being stranded sucked, especially when he had several articles he needed to read before reporting for work tomorrow.

He climbed into the cabin and put his bag on the floor. Turning to her, he waited until she was seated and reached for her seatbelt. "I'm Dan. And you're Amy?"

"S'pose Mark told you. I'm surprised you noticed my face."

"Look, I'm sorry I laughed. I didn't intend to embarrass you." Another woman would have laughed off the incident, or played it up. Amy's response suggested she lacked confidence.

Not his problem.

In the soft glow of the dashboard light, her chin tipped higher and her knuckles tightened on the wheel. "Can we not mention that again?" She pulled out onto the highway.

"Consider the subject closed." But Amy was mistaken if she thought he'd forget her. He folded his arms across his chest and closed his eyes.

Thirty minutes later, lulled by the motion of the car and several poor nights' sleep, Dan woke with a start as Amy pulled into the first service station on the way into town. He sat up and rubbed the back of his neck.

"I've got to pick up a few groceries. Where do you want me to drop you off?" She opened her door and jumped out before turning and pinning him with her hazel gaze.

"Uh, I can catch a taxi from here."

Amy nodded, rummaged in the side pocket of the door and took out a business card, which she passed across the centre console. "If you're sure. That's for a towing company. Ask Derro to organise a tow for your car in the morning. Night."

Dan looked at the card before opening his door. "Thanks for the ride." He shoved the card in his shirt pocket, grabbed his bag and made for the taxi rank across the side street without looking back.

Under other circumstances, he might have asked Amy out to dinner. Just to say thanks. But she'd made it clear she didn't want to see him again. Which would make tomorrow very interesting.

Chapter Two

Amy finished her pre-flight checks on Jessie's Girl as someone climbed aboard the Beechcraft favoured by the Royal Flying Doctor Service. The new doctor was on time, a point in his favour. She clipped her pen onto the clipboard and slipped out of her seat on the left of the cockpit.

First impressions were so important. Straightening her brand new captain's bars, she stepped into the main cabin. The doctor had his back to her, squatting as he added a box to the lowest storage cabinet. Faded blue jeans lovingly moulded his backside, which rested on a pair of well-worn work boots.

Amy tipped her head, admiring the view and wondering about the face beneath the dark brown hair curling onto his collar. He stood and turned in an athletic movement that barely gave her any time to hide her scrutiny.

"Morning, Amy." A pair of sea-blue eyes looked into hers and a half-smile flashed across his face before his expression returned to neutral. He offered a hand. "Dr Dan Middleton, reporting for duty."

Shit, shit, shit. Dan from last night, the 'perv' she'd chipped for ogling her, had caught her out. She waited for the gloating to begin.

And waited.

Dan opened his mouth and she stiffened her spine. Whatever he dished out, she deserved. Double standards hadn't been tolerated at home and she wasn't about to let them intrude at work.

"Can you talk me through the preparations for this morning, captain? I've read up on everything but I'd appreciate your input." Dr Dan's gaze remained neutral but . . . something—appreciation, maybe—flickered through his eyes.

Captain? Formality didn't cut it here in the Isa, but warmth trickled through her at his use of her rank.

"Certainly, Doctor, although we don't stand on ceremony. Just Amy is fine."

"Dan."

"Pardon?"

"Just Amy and Dan. Not doctor. So, give me your perspective on our work. I'm here to learn."

Amy shuffled her feet and hoped like hell he didn't know this was her first flight in the captain's seat. Within the rules, the plane and passengers were hers to command. Including Dr Dan. For the first time this weekend, her smile reasserted itself. "It'll be a pleasure Doc—Dan."

Her smile charged the air, crackled around Dan and lit up the cabin. And contrary to expectation when he heard she was his pilot, her uniform accentuated her femininity. After Mike's revelation, 'she's your pilot' had throbbed through his dreams alongside images of her glorious curves.

Knowing who Amy was, Dan had assumed she would also know him, which made her animosity last night appear rude and unpromising for their working relationship. It was the second reason for his poor sleep. Another toxic female with a grudge against him would stress anyone.

And yet today, she'd seemed surprised to see him. Mike's throwaway comment had prepared Dan for Amy's appearance from the cockpit. But maybe nobody had bothered to enlighten her about the identity of her medical partner. Last night's animosity might have nothing to do with knowing his background and everything to do with feeling embarrassed by her accidental flashing. The tension in his neck eased. Just maybe, he could get a fresh start here in the north west.

Amy led the way into the back of the cabin and Dan allowed his gaze to drop for the first time since boarding. Black trousers outlined her curves and highlighted a small waist. 'A waste of a waist' as Grandpa often remarked when he tucked Grams in for a hug. Amy was built on similar lines to his grandmother, petite but with feminine curves.

Dan bit back a groan and wondered which gods he'd pissed off. Assuming his flight team would be male had been sexist, but he'd hoped for one less stress factor after Gosford. Amy was not only all female but a very attractive woman.

"Are you okay?"

"What? Yes, why?"

"You groaned. Too much grog yesterday?"

"Not enough sleep." Dan cleared his throat and clapped a tight lid on his straying thoughts. Appreciation of the feminine was a no-go area. Strictly business and patient care from now on. "Please continue. You were telling me about the pickup procedure."

Amy followed Dan out of the hangar into the golden afternoon. All day, he'd listened, asked intelligent questions, and been thoroughly professional. And when they signed out, he offered a respectful, "Thanks, Captain Just Amy. Appreciate the introduction." Then he turned and headed onto the apron.

'Captain'. The acknowledgement sent tingles up her spine and left a warm afterglow. None of the other men had said a word about her new status. Before she changed her mind, she jogged after him.

"Hey, Dan, want a drink? My shout to welcome you."

The low sun silhouetted Dan as he turned back to her. He didn't answer immediately and suddenly she wished she could see his expression.

"Thanks, Amy, but I've got medical journals to catch up on." He strode through the gate into the staff car park. Not even a 'some other time' to make her feel better about her offer.

Her happy glow faded quicker than an ice cube at a summer barbeque. Shoving her hands into her pockets, she kicked a tuft of grass that dared to grow in a crack. Sure, Dan had been professional and polite all day. He even seemed to enjoy her company, which had led to her letting down her guard and inviting him out. Okay. So they were colleagues and a team on the job. Off the clock, separate lives. Check. Message received loud and clear. She hooked her thumbs through her belt tabs and strolled towards the car park.

Johnno's dual cab reversed out from a space several up from hers and pulled up beside her. Mike leaned out the passenger window and thumped the side panel. "Hey, Ames, jump in. We're going to The Tavern for a couple of coldies."

"Yeah, sure, why not." She squeezed into the back of the cabin and tugged the door shut behind, and sat with one hip on the armrest and one cheek on the seat. Reaching for her seat belt, she tugged it down and held it in her right hand so it appeared from the outside that she was legally buckled in. Unless she was prepared to put up with ribald comments from Dave on Trev's other side, the rest of her seatbelt would remain lost beneath Trev's generous butt.

As Johnno turned into the driveway of their local and drove over a speed bump, Amy hit her head. She rubbed the sore spot and let go of the seat belt. "Think you're Peter Brock at Mount Panorama, hey Dave?"

He pulled into a parking spot beneath a tree and killed the engine. "He was my hero. Gotta keep the memory alive."

Amy backed out of the cabin and led the way into the bar. Pool tables surrounded by off duty workers created an obstacle course. Amy followed the tiled perimeter to the bar, still three deep in thirsty men.

"Ames, grab us a table and I'll get the first round." Johnno gave her a gentle push towards the tables.

"Okay. Come on, Mike." Amy scanned the rapidly filling dining area. On the far side, one larger table was still free. Aware of another figure heading in the same direction, she walked briskly and plopped down on the bench seat against the brick wall.

Mike remained standing and waved someone over. "Hoy, doc. Wanna join us?"

Amy glanced across the next table to see which doctor Mike had spotted.

Dan? Her nails dug into her palms as annoyance sucked out her good humour. What had been so wrong with her invitation that Dan refused point blank? Yet here he was, smiling at Mike as he ambled over with a beer in hand.

Smiling at Mike?

She narrowed her eyes as her mind ticked over and she put two and two together. If she added in Dan's reluctance to engage with the women at work . . .

Oops. How had she not picked up the vibes? And while it was disappointing, it explained Dan's attitude to her. Not that any of the men at work looked at her with interest anyway. But after the heartache of Derek dumping her, she'd kind of hoped that maybe— just once—she might not be merely one of the boys. Was that why she'd dolled herself up for the Cloncurry Races?

As Dan's gaze met hers, his smile faded. "Just Amy, hi."

"It's okay, Dan. You don't need to worry anymore. I get it."

Mike looked from Amy to Dan. "Ignore her, mate. She goes troppo every so often. Not when she's flying of course—you're safe as a babe in the air with Tweety Bird. Sit with us anyway. Ames, I'm gonna order chips. Want some?"

"Yes, please."

Mike wandered over and joined the queue at the register. Dan slowly lowered himself onto a chair, watching her over the top of his beer, as though she was a time bomb about to explode. At least he was aware of her, which was a change from being seen as part of the furniture.

Some mischievous part of her decided to push his buttons—just a little. Just to let him know there were no hard feelings about his refusal. Now she understood why, reassurance sprang to her lips. "Noisy place to read those journals."

He placed a buzzer on the table and drew a deep breath. "Look, that was a nice gesture—the drink invite and all—but I do have a lot of reading to catch up on."

"You seemed pretty up to speed with operations stuff today. And the rest you'll learn on the job."

"Not good enough. My specialty is paediatrics but I hear there's been a few callouts to difficult births and I don't want to be underprepared."

Amy couldn't fault his logic, or his dedication to his work. "Last month, we had a pregnant mum go into premature labour on an isolated station."

"Exactly why I need to bone up on as much as I can."

"You could have told me, you know."

"What?"

"That you're a lousy cook." Idly, she set the food buzzer spinning.

"I heard the meals are pretty good here and I wanted a quick dinner before I hit the books. Why would you think I can't cook?"

"You mean you can? Of course you can. You probably have a really neat home too." Oops, she hadn't meant to let that stereotypical remark loose. Dan was a nice bloke, despite their less than stellar first meeting. "Sorry, what I meant to say was it doesn't matter that—"

Dan frowned and opened his mouth but Johnno plonked a tray with six beers in the middle of the table and the chance to talk about Dan's sexual preferences was lost. For the moment.

"There you go, doc. Welcome to The Isa." Johnno raised his glass and the others followed suit.

"Thanks. I'm glad to be here." Dan's buzzer flashed and edged towards the lip of the table like a possessed robot. He grabbed the device and, with an apology, jumped up to collect his meal.

"Nice bloke, our doc. Reckon he'll fit in well." Mike took a long pull of his beer.

Amy bit the inside of her cheek. Mike seemed oblivious to Dan's interest in him. But it wasn't her place to say anything. Grown men could sort themselves out, although Dan was going to be disappointed when he realised Mike's interest was solely in the female of the species.

"Hey, doc, any chance you can run Ames back to pick up her ute? The missus texted and I'll be in deep shit if I don't get home pronto." Johnno was already on his way, followed by Trev and the young apprentice, Dave.

"Uh, sure." Which left Dan with Amy and Mike. Safety in numbers stacked the odds in his favour.

Amy must have noticed his stunned mullet look. "Trev lives two doors down from Johnno, and Dave rides his bicycle to Johnno's and hitches a ride in to work. Johnno's wife is a fabulous cook. The only time he eats out is when she flies to Brisbane to visit family."

Dan made like a nodding toy as the wave of information washed over him. Wrapped in his own concerns and trying not to let his gaze stray below Amy's neck all day, he hadn't taken in much about his co-workers. His practice had always been to know at least the basics about fellow staff before he met them. Which showed how much the Gosford incident had rattled him. Mentally adding that task to his 'to do' list, he realised Amy had stopped talking and was watching him.

"Right. So, Mike, you'll be needing a lift too? Ready to go?" Dan pushed his chair back and looked down at the two of them. Mike and Amy seemed close. Maybe they were dating. And it was absolutely none of his business.

Mike grinned and leaned back on the bench seat. "Nah, all good. I'm heading up town. Meeting someone for—"

Amy lightly thumped Mike's arm. "Shush, too much information."

She turned to Dan and an expression that looked suspiciously like sympathy flitted across Amy's face. "Sorry, just you and me, Dan."

"No problem. Shall we?" He gestured for Amy to precede him. "Mike, can I drop by one night and we can continue our chat about fishing?"

"Sure, doc. Wednesday any good for you?"

"Yes, thanks."

Amy squirmed in the passenger seat. Should she warn Dan now or have a quiet word with Mike before Dan visited him? Give him a heads up. But could Mike be trusted to keep his mouth shut at work, or would Amy's good intentions make things difficult for Dan?

Settling on a friendly word to Dan, she turned to him as they pulled up at a set of traffic lights.

He looked at her. "Why Tweety Bird?"

That stupid nickname had haunted her since the day she'd bounced into Mike's workshop. Dressed in a yellow tank top, he claimed she'd twittered around him like a canary until he told her to find somewhere to perch and branded her forever. 'Sit—there—Tweety Bird.' Johnno heard him, and Trev, and others who had since moved on, and the name had stuck.

"It's not what you think."

"What do I think?"

"I'm not a bird brain. I just—talk a lot—sometimes."

"And here was me thinking it's because you're chirpy as in happy."

"The boys, well, Mike actually, called me that and—look, that's not what we should be talking about."

"Do you like being called Tweety Bird?"

"Truthfully? There are much worse names they could have come up with."

Amy was giving him the lowdown on the origins of Trev's 'Caper Cat' nickname when Dan pulled up beside her ute. "Look, I wanted to tell you about Mike before—"

Dan got out and came around to open her door. "Sorry, Amy, but I need to get home. I've set myself two chapters of reading per night for the next week. I don't want to be caught unprepared. Got your keys?"

She nodded and fished them out of her pocket. "Yep."

"See you in the morning." Dan lowered himself into his seat and, with a quick wave, left her to her thoughts.

Amy watched his taillights disappear through the gates before climbing into her ute. Dan seemed to be a nice bloke, decent and committed to his work. As she slid her key into the ignition, she sighed. "Maybe I am Tweety Bird. I talked too much and didn't tell him what I meant to."

Chapter Three

"Amy?" Johnno's wife rounded the tail of the plane as Amy ducked out from checking the undercarriage.

"Hi Terri. Johnno's working in number two hangar. Do you want me to—"

"I came to see you. Do you have a minute?" Terri clutched her 'Blue Hawaii' tote bag in both hands. She licked her lips and looked around as though checking to see they were alone.

A sinking feeling lurched through Amy's stomach. Terri only ever came to the airport to visit Johnno when something big happened. She was one of the most confident women Amy knew but today, she appeared uncertain. "Sure. It's morning tea time somewhere, isn't it?"

Terri nodded and followed Amy as she led the way through the reception area into the lunchroom. Babbling on like the Tweety Bird Mike had named her, Amy's mind raced through possibilities. "Things are good between Johnno and you, aren't they?"

"What? Yes. I adore the man, when I don't want to throttle him, and he adores me. And my cooking. Why?"

"You usually call in on Johnno, not me. Spill, what's up?"

"Ah, yes. Well,"—she fiddled with her bag, finally setting it on the floor between their two chairs and clasping her hands—"it's a favour I'm asking from you, a pretty big one. Did you know I've been asked to organise this year's RFDS fundraiserspecial?"

"They couldn't have asked a better person! But it's a huge job. Of course I'll help."

"Can I quote you?"

Relieved that her best friends were not in difficulty, words flew out of Amy's mouth. "Sure. What do you need?"

"Remember, you offered without hearing details first—I'm doing a theatre restaurant and I want you to organise a skit."

Like a stunned mullet, Amy froze. Drama in school had been an ordeal, and she'd opted to work backstage away from the attention. "You wouldn't ask if you'd been there when the flat I was propping up toppled during Sharyn's solo in 'Grease'. Madam was not impressed. She was singing about the worst things she could do when I fell at her feet."

Terri's hoot of laughter drew Amy's attention from the humiliating memory of the end of year musical. "Oh, gosh, if you could see your face!"

"You were kidding, right? Tell me you weren't serious."

"Oh, I'm serious all right. But you don't have to star onstage—just convince others to be in it. And write the script. And pour wine into me when I look desperate."

The door opened and closed as someone entered the lunch room. "Sounds like a con job being planned. Hi, how are you, Terri?" Dan threw her a smile and headed straight for the coffee pot and poured a mug.

"I'm enlisting Amy's help for the fundraiser I told you about last night. Care to help me out here, Dan?" Terri grinned at him then winked at Amy.

Dan pulled out a chair and eyed Amy over the top of his mug. "What did you think of Terri's idea?"

"The look on her face was priceless." Terri turned a fierce look on Amy. "And you agreed and I'm holding you to it."

"No problem, Terri." Sweet talk and charm weren't Amy's forte but she hoped Dan might be persuaded to help, given how well he seemed to get on with Terri. In fact, he was charming with all the married women on base. But watching him smile at Terri, Amy imagined herself caught in no-man's land. Dan was pleasant on the job, and supportive, but the shutters came down and he locked himself away from anything remotely personal with her and all the single women. Most of whom had cast interested looks his way. At least she knew why he didn't return their interest.

"Dan, how would you like to tread the boards in a good cause?"

A lazy, toe-curling smile tipped up one corner of his mouth. "Hey, I've already volunteered to do the music. Get yourself another playmate."

Playmate? If only. But it was useless feeling sorry for herself. Dan was off the playmate menu, even if Amy had possessed the inclination to attract his attention. No, friendship was all that was on offer and the thought made her feel better. That she had even considered Dan as playmate material meant she was getting over Derek and his bruised ego. "Okay, so maybe you can help me brainstorm ideas for this skit Terri has landed on me."

"Comedy? Melodrama? Musical?" A small frown drew Dan's eyebrows together as he drank more coffee. "What about a 'Flying High' skit? Remember the medical scene with an IV drip and a nun singing or something? You could play with that."

"Actually, that's a clever idea. Don't suppose you'd like to give me a hand scripting our version since you're Mr Music?"

Terri pulled a notebook from her tote and set it on the table. Elvis' face smiled from the cover above a Hawaiian shirt. She flipped the book open to a blank page before meeting Amy's gaze. "What about a scene from 'Blue Hawaii'? You could convince some of the girls to do a hula without much trouble. Bikinis and grass skirts would go well with the theme for the evening."

"And that's what precisely?" Amy would lay good odds on Terri bringing Elvis in somehow. She'd been in love with him since forever.

"Well, I love the idea of a luau style evening and I thought maybe—"

"'Blue Hawaii'." Both Amy and Dan chorused.

Terri's cheeks coloured. "Is that too naff? I thought costumes would be easy and casual, and catering it will be fun. I've got ideas already for decorations."

"You're the expert on all things Elvis and the theme sounds great. The skit doesn't have to be about the 'Flying Doctor'." Amy had watched a few old Elvis films with Terri when Johnno wasn't around. Girls' nights in usually ended that way.

Dan rose and rinsed out his mug. "Great planning, Terri. I'll download appropriate Hawaiian music and put together a few musical sets. Let me know if you decide to include a limbo competition or whatever." He headed for the door.

Amy jumped to her feet. "And help me script the skit? Please, Dan."

"Why me? I'm not an Elvis fan. Wouldn't Terri have more ideas?"

Amy ran her tongue over her lips. Poor Dan. His hands gripped the back of the chair while his gaze flicked between her and Terri. Was it the idea of being alone with a single woman that unsettled him?

"Sorry, I didn't mean to co-opt you like that but if it's a musical skit, I need your input. We could meet at Terri's house."

"Can I get back to you? I've got a meeting upstairs. Bye, ladies." Dan strode away leaving Amy bemused. Terri covered her mouth and suddenly appeared to find her notes intensely interesting.

The aroma of lamb casserole cooking filled the kitchen as Amy poured a glass of iced water. Dan was due any minute and she suspected Terri's offer of a home cooked dinner was only part of the reason.

Terri closed her phone. "Amy, love, I'm sorry but I'll be back as soon as I can." Terri grabbed her car keys from the hook and headed towards the garage.

"Don't worry, we can dine out for months on Johnno, the mechanic, breaking down a few miles from town. Dan won't turn tail and run because you're not here and we're alone together. In your house. Or maybe he will."

Dan had barely spoken two words to her since morning tea yesterday. Although he'd been trading quips with Trev in the workshop this morning, as soon as Amy appeared, he'd gone quiet and excused himself soon after. Swinging between amusement and annoyance, Amy shrugged.

Terri tipped her head to the side and opened her mouth, then snapped it shut. "Help yourself to the casserole. Johnno's idea of 'a couple of miles north of town' could be anything from two to twenty. Hopefully, I won't be too long." She pulled the door closed behind her and a minute later, Amy heard the sound of her car reversing up the drive.

"Great. Now to convince Doctor Dan this twosome isn't a plot and I'm not planning an assault on his person." Muttering aloud, Amy wandered into the back garden and flopped onto a pool lounger. Heat rose from the pavers and she toed off her sandals and looked longingly at the pool. Her bikini and towel were in her tote bag inside the house but the thought of greeting Dan in that undressed state sent a shiver down her spine.

She stretched her arms over her head and lay back, brushing a branch of grevillea that caught in her hair. Intending to move the lounger away from triffid plants, she swung her legs over the side and pushed up. But as she stood, she collided with a broad masculine chest. A girly shriek was cut off as she swept a leg behind her attacker and dropped him.

"Oof! What're you doing? It's me." Sprawled flat on his back, Dan looked up at her. Unable to say who was more surprised, heat crawled up Amy's cheeks. In the mortification stakes, she was definitely the winner.

"Oops, sorry." Her fingers closed over his forearms as she pulled him to his feet. He surged up, invading her space with his height and the scent of Cool Water. She stepped back and crashed into the lounger. Arms flailing, she overbalanced. Dan caught her hands and, in a heady moment of wish fulfilment, she was up close and personal, scenting his subtle cologne, so fresh and masculine she wanted to bury her nose in his neck.

Why did her meetings with him always start with her embarrassing herself in some way? Pushing away from his chest, she knew the heat in her cheeks was visible to him. "I didn't hear you. Are you okay?"

He released her and stooped to pick up the wine cooler he'd been carrying. "I'm fine. I rang the doorbell. When there was no answer, I thought you might be poolside so I came down the side of the house. Is Terri inside?" With measured steps, he put distance between them and placed the cooler on the glass-topped table before he moved to stand behind a single outdoor chair.

Amy pushed her hair off her forehead and sat on the edge of the lounger. "Johnno's car is broken down north of town and she's gone to pick him up. They shouldn't be long but she said to help ourselves to dinner. Would you like—?"

"I don't mind waiting, unless—"

"No, I'm fine. So, do you want to get down to it? I mean— Gah! That did not come out right." With a groan, she hid her face in her hands.

A rich baritone laugh erupted, the first she'd heard from Dan. The sound was smooth and sweet, like her favourite Benedictine liqueur. Sneaking a peek between her fingers, she caught her breath. He was an attractive man—ask any of the women on base—but when he laughed, his face came alive. Laugh lines bracketed his mouth and his eyes crinkled. He was handsome, and so very appealing when he relaxed his guard.

And so unavailable.

Sighing with frustration, she reined in her appreciation before she let it gallop away.

"Tweety Bird, I would love to get down to it—on your script. Want a wine while we work?"

She nodded and jumped up. "I'll get a couple of glasses."

In the kitchen, she leaned her forehead against the cupboard and drew a deep breath. What unlucky star had she been born under? Other women didn't make strings of gaffes like she did. She thumped her head against the cabinet before opening the door and taking down two wineglasses.

By the time she returned, Dan had set two chairs at the table and fired up his laptop. He twisted the cap off the wine and showed her the label. "Do you like shiraz? Terri had this the other night when I called in."

"Yeah, we drink that or beer whenever we're here. Thanks." She held out a glass for Dan to fill and then set it on the table while he poured a drink for himself. "I'm really sorry about attacking you like that. If you'd called out or something—"

"Actually, I did call. But hey, don't be sorry. That's a really good move you have. If only more women took the initiative and learned self-defence, I reckon we'd see fewer casualties coming through the Emergency department." Dan raised his glass in a toast. "Well done, Tweety Bird."

"Thanks." What more could she say? Dan might not be into women and he might keep his distance but he made her feel good. Better than good. If she put aside the unreachable prospect of Dan as boyfriend material, there was potential for a real friendship between them. If only she could quell her attraction to him.

"Do you want to hear which songs I've pulled out of Terri's favourite film as possibilities for your skit? And may I add, this was a tough job."

"Because there were so many choices?" Amy chuckled at the thought of Johnno doing what Dan had done. As much as he loved Terri, watching an entire Elvis movie would be beyond him.

"Watching the whole thing was more than I could manage but this song looks promising." Dan clicked on a YouTube clip and through to a group scene of bikini-clad girls and young men on a beach. "If Terri is after a hula for the women, 'Ito Eats' fits the bill. And it would suit her luau theme."

As Amy watched, ideas tumbled from her brain and when the music ended, she touched Dan's arm and swivelled to face him. "Don't put yourself through any more torture. That's perfect."

Beneath her hand, his muscles tensed and Dan sat back. His arm slipped away from her touch and Amy's pleasure dimmed as she reminded herself he didn't welcome the touch of a woman.

Pinning a smile on her face, Amy picked up her wine and took a sip, fortifying herself for the discussion she knew they needed to have. "Look, Dan, can I clear the air with you?"

The wary look was back in his eyes, and his gaze darted to the house. "About what?"

"You're a really nice bloke and I like working with you but that's all there is to it. I'd like us to be friends, nothing more. No pressure, no expectations, just—mates."

Wariness gave way to a puzzled frown. "Why are you telling me this now?"

"I'm working in what some people still see as a man's world. I've just earned my captain's bars—"

"You mean to tell me—"

"You're my first doctor."

Dan's mouth quirked up in a one-sided smile Amy hoped to see more often. "Glad I didn't know our first flight together was your first in charge. I might have been tempted to—"

"Bail out? No deal, doc. You're stuck with me." Amy returned his smile and ploughed on. "So, can we put aside this male female thing and just be work colleagues and friends?"

"Amy, there are reasons why I maintain distance from the women at work."

"I get it. And I don't want to complicate a work relationship any more than you do. Just think of me like you do Johnno, or Mike or any of the other blokes. Except when it comes to which side of the plane is mine." She winked at him and was pleased to see the tension in Dan's body ease. This friend thing could even be fun if he wasn't worrying about what she might be after, and they could just enjoy one another's company.

The veranda light flicked on and the screen door banged against the wall. "We're home." Terri and a sheepish looking Johnno emerged through the back door. "Come on in and I'll serve dinner since it looks as though you two haven't touched the casserole. Is that shiraz you're drinking? Dan, you're a good man." Terri bustled back inside as Amy and Dan rose, scooping up the wine, glasses, and Dan's laptop.

"Hi, Johnno. How's the truck?" Amy led the way across the grass to the shallow steps into the house.

Johnno leaned against an upright, and rubbed the back of his neck. "Fan belt went and some silly coot had nicked the spare."

"Didn't you consider catching a snake to use?" Amy had babysat Terri and Johnno's two children the first night they watched 'Bran NueDae'.

Johnno grinned. "Ah, you don't believe what you saw in that movie, do you, Ames?"

"You'll have to teach me tips for driving out here. I haven't heard about the snake yet." Dan followed her inside, stowed his laptop and then topped up their glasses and poured one each for Terri and Dan. A second bottle appeared from his wine cooler as he joined them at the dining table.

They raised their glasses and Terri offered a toast. "Here's to a successful fundraiser, and thanks to wonderful friends for helping."

"And to one amazing lady with a vision and drive to succeed. Terri." Dan's words surprised Amy. Not because he'd acknowledged Terri's work but because the depth of his appreciation was unexpected.

Amy glanced at him as he replaced his glass and picked up his cutlery. He seemed more at ease than he'd been since his arrival. Maybe having Dan as her friend wouldn't be so hard after all.

Chapter Four

"Come on, it will be fun." Amy hadn't expected resistance from the office staff to her skit but it was proving to be a tough sell. "Hey, don't you want to show off those gorgeous bodies you've been toning up at your pole dancing classes?"

"We can't go from hula skirts to ball-level perfection again after your skit. And who wants to wear a coconut bra? Eww." Lizzy, one of Sharyn's Barbie-circle of friends idly filed her perfect manicure before pinning Amy with a glare.

"Wouldn't be fair on our dates either," Tess, the office junior, crossed her arms. Suddenly, her disinterest dissolved and a smile lit her face as she gazed past Amy's shoulder. Along with every other female in the room.

Amy didn't need a sixth sense to work out the reason. Silly women, falling all over themselves and making cow eyes at Dan. Of course, she wasn't hypersensitive. Just—aware when he was near. Like good team members should be aware of each other.

He leaned on the counter beside her and stage whispered. "We may have to divulge the theme—in secret, of course. Don't you think that might set a few minds at rest?"

Lizzy sashayed up to the counter opposite Dan. Ample cleavage showed as she leaned forward. "Do tell, Dan. What's the theme? I promise not to tell." She made a cross on her chest, drawing attention to the expanse of skin exposed by her low-cut V-neck, and simpered up at him.

Amy had to give him credit. His eyes never once strayed below Lizzy's face and he kept a pleasant expression on his face. "What do you think, Amy? Shall we spill the good news?"

"I think Terri should have the pleasure."

For a timeless moment, the others faded into oblivion as his sea-blue gaze met and held hers. Then Dan pulled his hand from behind his back, turned to the women and flourished a pile of posters. "Terri's just delivered these for us to put up around the base. Ladies, what do you think?" He held one up to show the office staff.

"Oh, cool! Hawaiian theme." Lizzy tapped Dan's arm and looked up from under coyly lowered lashes. "So, will the blokes come bare-chested? I love the idea."

"Anything's possible. Can you put these up around the office for Terri?" He handed over a few and added, "By the way, we need people to perform in a skit. Any chance—?"

"Absolutely. We wouldn't miss it, would we, Tess?"

Certain that Dan had heard the earlier comments, Lizzy's complete about-face would have been annoying if Amy hadn't seen the funny side. She bit down on her tongue to hold back the laughter bubbling up inside.

"Great, thanks." Dan turned to Amy and, with a swift wink for her alone, sauntered back into the workshop.

Amy tapped her short, mint-green-polished nails on the counter and watched Dan's exit. That was one way to achieve a goal. Since their dinner at Terri's, he'd eased off the 'iceman' image, although maybe it was a 'safety in numbers' approach. Once she had her face under control, she turned back to the women and nodded. "Okay, thanks for volunteering. We'll let you know when the first rehearsal will be."

Dan finished checking the contents of the medi-pack container and replaced it in the storage locker. The exercise occupied both hands and mind but was simple enough that his off-kilter response to Amy wouldn't affect the result.

Through the window he'd watched her standing her ground and trying to convince Tizzy Lizzy, the office Barbie—he grinned at the apt nickname Amy had let slip at Terri's—to help at the fundraiser. The woman seemed to have her claws out for Amy and be making it difficult for the others to join in. His grip had tightened on the bundle of posters and he'd stepped into the office, intending only to interrupt Lizzy's attack.

But as he stood beside Amy, the scent of her hair, like fresh apples, had distracted him and he'd all but forgotten why he was there. And when she turned her hazel gaze on him, his name deserted him. For the longest moment, they just stood . . .

'Friends'. Her words haunted him. Just mates and colleagues. But try as he may, he couldn't see her as one of the boys. Not when her ponytail bounced above the slim column of her neck, and her uniform hugged her curves and proclaimed her all woman. Sweet and feisty rolled into one. Nothing could come of the attraction. Amy had as good as told him that but his body didn't accept her declaration. And his head should know better too. After Gosford, there couldn't be any work-based relationship.

"Hey, doc, you in there?" Johnno poked his head through the doorway and climbed aboard.

"What's up?" Wiping a smear of dust from his hands, Dan moved into the main part of the cabin.

"Got a call out for you and Ames. She's getting the details now."

"Thanks. I've finished my stock take. All good to go." Mentally switching gears, Dan moved into his personal pre-flight checks.

Johnno glanced through the hatch and stood his ground, blocking the hatch, and pinned Dan with a look. "Before Ames gets here, I want a word with you. She's in a vulnerable place right now. Don't hurt her or you'll have me, and more frightening, Terri, to deal with."

"Hurt Amy? I have no intention of hurting her. What gave you the idea that—?"

"Terri. She reckons Ames likes you but she's coming off a broken relationship. Bastard dumped her when she was shortlisted for promotion and he wasn't."

Anger surged through Dan. How anyone could be stupid enough to throw away Amy's heart was beyond him. "If it sets your mind at rest, Amy told me she wants nothing more than to be friends. Not that I'd ask for more. I want a calm and comfortable workplace, that's all. No romance, no entanglements, no potential for disruption."

"Disruption? Ha! Lost that one the day you showed your face here, mate. Women in the office love single, handsome fellas like you." Johnno chuckled then straightened as Amy climbed aboard. "Keep that goal in mind, doc. Safe flight, Tweety Bird."

"Will do." Amy stood aside as Johnno jumped down the stairs and disappeared. "What was that about goals?"

"Bloke talk. What are the details on our call out?" Focusing on the job was a lot more comfortable than thinking about what Johnno had divulged. Or the fact that Amy was free. It simply meant he would have to be more vigilant and ensure nothing he did gave her the wrong idea. Which would be the right idea, only he refused to act on it. Gosford had seen to that.

Amy slipped into the left seat and read the information aloud as Greg, her co-pilot, arrived. "Broken leg and concussion. Remote location. The landing will be rough. Need to collect any supplies before we're cleared for takeoff?" Amy carried out thorough checks in her pre-flight, but her clipped question was dismissive and at odds with the sparks jumping between them in the office.

"No, I just finished checking supplies before the call out. All good to go." Interrupting her now wouldn't be helpful but Dan needed to know if he was the cause of her distance. He buckled his seatbelt and replayed their encounter while the plane taxied and leapt into the sky. But no matter how much he dissected it, nothing accounted for Amy's abrupt mood swing.

Troubled by Johnno's revelation, Dan stared through the porthole. Beneath them, dry, brown land gradually gave way to a winding river and steep-sided hills that would make rounding up livestock difficult.

"Keep your eyes open for orange smoke, doc." Greg's voice came through Dan's headset and pulled him back to the present.

Smoke canisters made finding patients in remote areas easier and quicker than spotting tiny figures from the plane.

Dan concentrated on scanning the ancient landscape. Time could be critical if the patient's concussion was bad.

"Portside, ten o'clock." Amy banked left and descended, lining up an approach between two columns of orange smoke rising almost vertically.

Dan could see nowhere to land but Amy approached with confidence. And then, the wheels touched down and they bumped over rough ground that jarred his teeth in his head. As the plane came to a standstill, he relaxed his white-knuckled grip on the armrest.

Amy was out of her seat and unlocking the hatch before he'd unbuckled. Her white face was set and her shoulders looked like she carried the weight of the world as she clattered down the steps.

Hampered by his medical bag and a medi-container, Dan followed as quickly as he could. Several stockmen stood in a semi-circle around one of their team. Ahead of him, Amy dropped to her knees by the patient's head, bent over him, and stroked his face. "Jeff, wake up."

As Dan reached the group and set down his gear, she looked up. Amy never cried but her eyes shimmered with unshed tears. "I can't get him to wake up. Oh please, Dan, do something. He's my brother."

Chapter Five

Amy couldn't stop the trembling in her hand. Jeff, bossy big brother and tower of strength, lay unmoving as she stroked his pale cheek. A thin trickle of blood seeped from his ear.

Dan bent over and checked Jeff's pulse and pupil dilation. After that, his actions blurred as she fought a losing battle and the tears rolled down her face. Impatiently, she wiped the back of her hand over her eyes.

"It's bad, isn't it, Dan?" She caught her lower lip between her teeth and sniffed. Damn the stupid tears. They wouldn't help Jeff and Greg might get the idea he should captain their return flight. Over her dead body. Nobody but her would be flying Jeff anywhere. She blinked away her tears and looked at Dan for any sign that the worst might happen.

"I've eased the pressure and his vitals are stable but it will be easier to assess him in hospital."

Dan's expression gave nothing away but his calm control steadied her and gave her hope. "What do you want me to do?"

"Prepare for takeoff while we move him onto the evac-board."

Leaving Jeff lying there pulled against every instinct. She sucked in a deep breath and forced herself to stand. "We'll be ready for takeoff as soon as you are, doctor." On unsteady legs, she ran back to the plane and climbed into her seat.

Fear like blinding fog wrapped around her and her heart pounded as though she'd run a marathon. What if they were too slow? What if Jeff didn't make it?

"Captain? Amy? I can fly home if you want to sit in the back with your brother." Concern tinged his voice and expression as Greg offered the tissue box.

A good co-pilot, Greg's notion of his skills didn't match with her perception. He flew well but the thought of his takeoff from this remote corner of her family's property was enough to drag Amy from her morbid speculation. One deep, steadying breath, and another, and she found her voice. "Thanks, Greg, that won't be necessary." She grabbed a couple of tissues and blew her nose defiantly.

Behind them, Jeff was being lifted into the cabin. Dan's authoritative voice gave directions and then the locks clicked into place. "Thanks, everyone."

Pete, who had carried her on his shoulders when she was knee-high to a grasshopper, gripped her shoulder and leaned forward. "Hey, Amy, he'll be okay with you flying him. Take care, love."

"Thanks, mate. Doctor Dan is good." Amy swallowed and prepared to turn and taxi.

Len, their head stockman paused in the hatchway. "Doc, let us know how Jeff's doing, will ya?"

"We'll get word to you when we know more." Dan shook hands with Len before shutting the hatch. As he stepped back, he caught her eye. "All set, Captain?"

"Yes, Doctor. Ready for takeoff." Her hands moved in automatic, familiar patterns as she turned the plane downhill and lined up her run. Increasing revs to maximum, she released the brakes. They bump-rolled down the emergency runway and skimmed the low, surrounding hills before climbing to cruising altitude.

Desperate to know how Jeff was progressing but torn with the need to maintain control of his lifesaving flight, Amy settled for a glance over her shoulder. Dan looked up, as though he sensed her unspoken question.

"He's doing okay, Amy. Stable for now. Have you requested an ambulance to meet us at the plane yet?"

Greg picked up the radio. "I'll make the call."

Amy nodded. "Thanks. And if you don't mind finishing the flight log, I'd like to go in the ambulance with him." Amy had never left any detail undone in her capacity as pilot but there was no way she was letting Jeff go without her. Their father was probably even now making the five-hour drive to Mt. Isa, anxious about the bare facts relayed to the homestead. When would her mother arrive back from a visit to her sister's at Caloundra?

Preoccupied with her worries, time slipped away and before she knew it, the smokestack and airport came into view. Greg radioed in and requested priority clearance.

The Tower's reply was quick. "Romeo Foxtrot Delta cleared to land, runway 22, report clear of runway."

Amy concentrated, using all her skill to land as gently as possible. Her brother's life was in her hands. Minutes later, they touched down and taxied to the ambulance. She powered down, and handed over control. "All yours, Greg. Thanks."

Dan oversaw Jeff's transfer to the waiting ambulance and then turned to offer her a hand into the vehicle. "Come on, Amy. Sit here beside your brother and talk to him."

Amy shuffled past Dan and took a seat near Jeff's head. She picked up her brother's hand and squeezed gently. "Jeff? It's Amy. We'll be at the hospital soon. Dad's driving in. He'll be here soon. You know what Rory will say about you falling off your horse, don't you? You're never going to hear the end of it."

The ambulance doors closed and Dan seated himself facing the monitors attached to her brother. At regular intervals, Dan checked Jeff's vital signs but somehow never intruded on Amy's space as she talked about their family and the property.

"Do you think he can hear me?"

Dan's gaze connected with hers and he nodded. "I believe it helps."

##

Dan glanced at the clock on his bedside table. Five-thirty on a muggy morning. He threw off the sheet, and rubbed his gritty eyes before heading to the kitchen for a cold milk drink. Last night's plans to continue his study of breech births had been shelved the moment he realised his patient was Amy's brother. Dimly, Dan recalled mention of her family living on a property. Wrapped in his own concerns, he hadn't connected the call out location with the sparse details of Amy's family home. In truth, they'd spoken little about their families, which suited Dan just fine. Leaving the past where it belonged meant he didn't have to discuss Gosford.

Jeff Alistair had been returned to a private room after surgery and Amy refused to leave his side until she knew he was stable. Dan had waited with her until her father texted to say that he'd arrived at the hospital. Leaving father and daughter to meet in private, Dan returned home. Sleep proved elusive as the memory of Amy's white face and trembling fingers brushing her brother's pale cheek played on loop, followed by the image of her conquering her fear to fly her brother to hospital. His admiration for both her skill, and her quiet strength had grown as she refused to give in to fear.

Glancing at the time, he decided it was irrelevant. The sun was up and he doubted whether Amy or her dad had broken their vigil over their brother and son. He dressed quickly, grabbed his keys and headed out to find an open bakery.

There was never a quiet time at a major hospital but, at this early hour, finding a parking spot was easier. He tapped on the door of the private room and pushed it open quietly. Amy and her father looked up, fatigue written on both faces.

Dan placed the tray of takeaway coffee and a bag of fresh bakery croissants on the tray table. "Grab some caffeine. Has he woken yet?"

Amy shook her head. "Dan, this is my dad, Gareth. Dad, Dan is the doctor who looked after our Jeff." Her voice was husky from more than lack of sleep and Dan fought an urge to fold her in his arms.

Gareth Alistair pushed to his feet. Tall and rangy, he looked Dan in the eye and held out his hand. "Dan, thanks for what you did for Jeff."

"Just doing my job, Gareth. I'll check his chart."

"Thanks for breakfast." Gareth carried his coffee and a croissant to the window and stood looking outside while he ate.

Dan picked up the charts from the end of the bed and flipped through the night's data. "He's stable. That's good. And the surgery report is encouraging. Has the doctor been around yet?"

"No. Is that good or bad?" Dark shadows highlighted Amy's fatigue and she swayed a little as she looked over his arm at the charts.

"Neither. It just means he hasn't done his rounds yet. Amy, how about you and your dad head into the visitors' room for a break? There's a couch and a comfortable armchair where you might grab an hour or two of sleep."

"I can't leave Jeff. What if he wakes up and we're not here?"

"I'll wait with him while you nap. If you like. Sorry, I don't mean to intrude but you look like you're out on your feet."

She touched his arm. "Thanks, Doctor Dan, but I need to stay with him. Talk to him. You were the one who said you believe it helps. If there's nothing else I can do for him, I can at least sit and talk. I'm Tweety Bird, remember?" Her half smile didn't quite reach her eyes and suddenly, the reason for her huskiness made sense.

Dan covered her hand with his. "You talked to him all night, didn't you? I can talk to him if you like. Tell him about the wonderful job you did. That was great flying, Just Amy. That landing strip was almost as scary as some I encountered in PNG."

"When were you in PNG?" Gareth pitched his empty coffee cup into the bin and joined them, folding his arms across his chest.

Dan released Amy's hand and shoved his hands in his pockets. "I did a term working in a mountain clinic inland from Rabaul. Do you know the area?" Few people Dan had met were keen to visit, let alone work in, the wild country on Australia's northern border but he'd been drawn to the volunteer program over the uni summer break.

"I spent a couple of years in the late seventies working with a friend of my father's on his property on the east coast. They were experimenting with cross breeding cattle at the time. Beautiful country but dangerous in more ways than one. We had some hair-raising flights in those days."

A soft groan drew the three of them to Jeff's bedside. Amy and her dad spoke his name together while Dan took his pulse and watched as his eyelids fluttered open. Jeff's Adam's apple bobbed up and down and he licked dry lips. "Water."

"Use a straw." Dan nodded to the tray on which a plastic water jug, glass and two straws sat.

Amy poured half a glass and popped a straw from its paper covering before holding it close to her brother's mouth.

"Thanks, Ames." Jeff flicked a glance at his sister before his eyelids closed again.

"How are you feeling, son?" Gareth touched his son's shoulder.

With what was clearly an effort, Jeff turned his head and squinted at his father. "I've had worse days. Can't think of one right now—"

The door squeaked as it was pushed open and Dan turned as the surgeon walked in. "Dr Harper, good morning."

Harper greeted Jeff's family then met Dan's gaze. "How's our patient this morning, Dr Middleton?"

"He woke a few moments ago and recognised his family." Unspoken, they shared the tacit knowledge that both had been concerned about the length of time Jeff Alistair had been out for the count.

Laurence Harper checked the obs before conducting his own physical examination. He finished checking Jeff's pupil dilation, before addressing Gareth Alistair. "With rest and time, I believe your son will make a complete recovery. He's lucky Dr Middleton got to him so quickly. And that your men didn't attempt to move him after his horse threw him. If they had, I'm not sure he'd be with us now."

Amy choked back a gasp, her breath loud in the quiet room. "Oh, my God." She slipped into the chair beside the bedside table, picked up her brother's hand and raised it to her lips.

A single tear slid down her cheek and she brushed it away with the back of her hand.

Dan had never wanted to offer comfort so much as right now. To hold her in his arms and kiss away the tears he suspected she rarely allowed to fall. To let her know he was there for her.

"It will be good if your brother sleeps now, Amy. Why don't you and your father do the same?" Dr Harper replaced the clipboard on the hook at the end of Jeff's bed. With a smile and a nod, he continued his rounds.

"Amy, come on, love. We'll catch a taxi home and catch some shut-eye. We won't be any use to Jeff if we're out on our feet." Gareth gently urged his daughter to her feet.

"I've got my car here. I'd be happy to drop you off, and, Amy, if you like, I can let work know you won't be in today." Dan opened the door as father and daughter left with backward glances at the man they'd almost lost.

"That's kind of you, Dan. Thanks." Amy hooked her arm through her father's and walked slowly along the corridor.

He doubted they would wait for evening before they'd be back.

Amy pulled her front door open and followed Dan onto the veranda. Inside, the microwave pinged as her father made a bowl of porridge. "Appreciate the ride home, Dan."

How could she let him know how grateful they were? Not for the ride but for the gift of her brother's life. Without Dan's skill and early intervention, Jeff might have been lost to them.

Dan stood looking at her, his blue eyes dark like a stormy sea. As though he wanted to say something. With a slight shake of his head, he turned to leave.

"Dan?" Maybe her guard was down, maybe it was fatigue talking, but she touched his arm and, when he turned back, reached up and kissed him.

Only her aim was off. Or maybe it was her subconscious guiding her. Instead of his cheek, she kissed his lips. As kisses go, it was the merest brushing of lips, soft and light, and over in a second.

So why had she forgotten how to breathe? Why couldn't she release her hold on his arm?

Why was Dan standing frozen to the spot like some clothed statue of David?

And how could she deny herself the chance to taste him again? Coffee and cologne mingled as she leaned towards him and closed her eyes.

"Amy? Breakfast's ready, love." Her father's voice shattered the spell and the moment was gone. Her eyes opened and she dropped her hand as Dan stepped away.

"I've got to get to work." Dan jumped down the three steps onto her brick path and strode to his car. He drove off without looking back, merging with the morning traffic and disappearing even as her dad stepped onto the veranda.

"Come on in, love. Porridge is on the table and then we'll both try to sleep for a while." He slung an arm around her shoulder and drew her into his side. "He's an impressive young man, your Doctor Dan. I like him."

"He's not my anything, Dad. You've got the wrong end of the stick."

Gareth gazed at his daughter before dropping a kiss on her forehead. "You could have fooled me, love. But, mum's the word."

Chapter Six

"You've got a pick up, Dan. Since Amy's off, Greg will be your pilot." Lizzy handed him the slip and leaned on the counter.

"What about a co-pilot?" Dan glanced at the information and considered whether to add anything to his supplies.

"Nothing unusual about the job, and it's an easy run. Greg is up to it. So—how is Amy this morning?" There was something odd in the smirk on Lizzy's face. Behind her, Tess covered a giggle with a fake cough.

Dan frowned. What was he missing here? Clearly there was a subtext but for the life of him, he couldn't work it out.

Lizzy's expression morphed into one of concern. "So awful about her brother's accident, wasn't it?"

"It was touch and go for a while last night. Amy and her father spent the night at the hospital. I called in this morning and drove them home."

"They were? You did? I thought— I mean, that's tough." For the first time since he'd met her, Lizzy blushed and lowered her lashes. "Please tell her I'm thinking of her when you see her."

"Why don't you drop in yourself and tell her. I expect she'd appreciate that." Without waiting for a response, Dan headed out to meet Greg at the plane. It would be odd flying without Amy but after that kiss—that accidental kiss—he wasn't sure he could face her today.

"Hey, doc, ready to go?" Greg's grin was wider than the hangar doors. "I'll be your pilot today, captain of my own airship. Cool, huh?"

"Yes, cool. Give me five minutes to grab some extras from Supply."

"Aren't we fully stocked already?"

"Just in case. We're picking up an expectant mother. She's not quite due but I want to be prepared for anything." Dan's study had given him a new appreciation of the many things that could go wrong in the late stages of pregnancy and peace of mind came with knowing he had everything covered. Well, almost everything.

By the time he returned, Greg had completed his pre-flight checks and they taxied to the waiting area at the far end of the runway to wait for their clearance.

Seated in the right hand seat in the cockpit, Dan tried to relax but the memory of Amy's kiss thrummed through him. There was no point reading more into it than there was. Amy had been absolutely clear they were no more than friends. Colleagues and mates. Maybe she'd been about to kiss his cheek. Sleepless nights and fear for her brother must have thrown off her aim.

And who could say whether his subconscious hadn't tempted him to turn his head at the last moment so she connected with his mouth? But the brush of her lips on his had broken through the barrier he'd erected and left him wanting more. Much more.

Desperately rationalising further, if he was honest, what they'd shared wasn't truly a kiss. It was more like the promise of one. A sweet, soft temptation that he couldn't—must not—give into. Not if he wanted to remain with the RFDS. And yet . . .

Kissing Amy—properly kissing her—occupied his thoughts until Greg's voice through the headset roused him from his internal debate. There could be no winners in the situation.

Shelving further thoughts of Amy, Dan looked around as Greg landed on the graded strip and taxied towards a four-wheel drive parked near the end. He cut the engines and Dan climbed out to greet the man leaning against the vehicle.

"G'day. Mr Campbell? Where's our patient?" Dan glanced into the vehicle, expecting to see the woman sheltering in the shade.

"She's fine. She doesn't need to go to hospital. Sorry for the inconvenience but she's not going with you." Unexpectedly surly, the man planted his feet wide and folded his arms across his chest.

"There must be some mistake. Base received a request from"— Dan fished the slip of paper from his pocket and checked the name—"a Donna Campbell asking to be transported to Mt. Isa because she can't travel by road. Is that your wife, sir?" Dan held the paper out but the man ignored it.

"She's my wife and she doesn't need to go anywhere. Baby can be born here, just like all of us were. We don't need the Flying Doctor."

"Sir, your wife called us to pick her up. Look, how about you take us up to the house and I can at least examine her?" Vibes pinging off the man raised the hairs on the back of Dan's neck. Behind him, Dan could hear Greg clattering down the stairs.

Campbell looked from Dan to the plane. His eyes narrowed. "Sure, why not come up to the house and check her out. You'll see. She's fine. Hop in." He jerked a thumb at the four-wheel drive.

"I'll let my pilot know what's happening." Dan took a couple of steps backwards. He'd eat his hat, as Grandpa said, if something wasn't going on.

"Tell him to come along. Might as well have a cuppa while he's waiting." Campbell got into his car and slowly rolled towards the plane, braking a few metres behind Dan.

Greg sheltered in a sliver of shade cast by the plane. He glanced past Dan's shoulder. "Where's the patient?"

"Radio base. The husband seems disinclined to allow his wife to come with us but she was the one who radioed for a pick up. We may be longer than expected."

"What do you want to do, doc?" Greg checked his watch. "Do you reckon we'll be back before dinner? I've got a date I want to keep."

"I hope so, Greg. Let base know I'm going to make a house call and see what's going on for now. I'll assess how both baby and mother are and ascertain whether a home birth is the mother's choice first. Tell them we'll radio again after I've seen the patient." Dan climbed aboard and collected his gear, and added the supplies he'd brought aboard as a precaution. The husband's determination to put off the Flying Doctor raised a flag that Dan couldn't ignore.

Greg signed off from his call to base and joined Dan. "Hopefully the homestead isn't far."

Dan handed over the second medi-container and led the way down the steps. "And hopefully our patient can clear up the miscommunication between her call to us and her husband's unwillingness to let her fly."

A short drive along an unsealed track led to a sprawling cluster of old buildings. A wide veranda sheltered all four sides of the house, creating deep shadows beneath the glare of the midday sun. Behind the house, an ancient windmill clanked and turned in the occasional breeze. Campbell pulled up beside the house and a trio of working dogs barked from the other side of a high fence that surrounded the homestead garden. Of his wife, there was no sign.

"Come on in."

Dan and Greg collected the equipment and Campbell led the way, holding a screen door open for them to precede him into a wide hallway that bisected the house.

"Which way?"

A high-pitched scream had him sprinting down the hallway into a small room furnished with an old-fashioned cot and rocking chair. A young woman sat in the chair and clutched her stomach. At her feet, a pool of water splotched with blood told him the woman had been right to call for help. He squatted beside her and gently touched her shoulder.

"Donna, I'm Dan, the Flying Doctor. I've come to help you have your baby. Can you stand and walk?"

Donna sucked in a breath and opened her eyes. She nodded and, taking the arm he offered, struggled to her feet. A small, relieved smile replaced the grimace of pain and she leaned close. "Thank you for coming, doctor. I was afraid—"

Campbell stepped into the room.

Beneath Dan's fingers, Donna's muscles tensed and he slipped an arm around her back. But the contraction he's expected didn't happen.

She leaned into Dan's side and clutched his free hand as she glanced up at her husband. "Jebediah. My baby's coming early." For a woman in labour, Donna's voice lacked either excitement or fear.

He put the impression aside for later consideration. "You can tell me what happened while we walk to your bedroom." He locked gazes with Jebediah Campbell in the doorway. "While I examine your wife, I need you to call the RFDS base. Let them know we'll be in touch when I know what stage of labour your wife is in, and whether she'll need to be admitted to hospital."

Jebediah glared at his wife and a muscle spasmed in his jaw. Without a word, he turned away and disappeared into a room on the opposite side of the house.

Another contraction shuddered through Donna and she sagged in Dan's hold. "Greg, come around the other side and help me get Donna into a bedroom. Then go and see if her husband needs assistance getting through to base."

As the contractions eased, they walked Donna down the hallway and turned into the room she indicated. The ironwork bedhead looked as if it was as old as the homestead. As they lowered Donna onto the mattress, the creaking noises confirmed the bed was an original item of furniture.

"Need anything else, doc?" Looking pale around the gills and rather less cocksure than usual, Greg edged towards the door.

"Just make sure base knows we have a situation and we'll be in touch ASAP. You'll be fine, Donna." As Greg hastily removed himself from what had become an impromptu birthing room, Dan took his stethoscope from his personal medical bag and hung it around his neck.

"Now, can you tell me why your husband doesn't want you to fly to Mt. Isa?" As he checked Donna's blood pressure, out of the corner of his eye, Dan watched her eyes dart to the door. "It's okay. He won't be back for a few minutes."

His hand was gripped with surprising strength and she tugged him close and whispered. "He thinks I won't come back with the baby." Another contraction stole her breath.

"Pant, don't push, Donna. I'm going to check how far dilated you are and see how your baby is positioned. Okay?" When the contraction eased and she could relax, Dan pulled on a pair of surgical gloves to examine her.

Reluctantly, she raised her soaked dress to her waist. "It hurts so much, Doctor."

"Call me Dan." He smiled and bent his head to begin his examination and froze.

Bruises covered her hips, some faded to yellow-green splotches, others, angry purple and new. Anger surged within him like a tidal wave and he gritted his teeth as he desperately sought control. Donna needed calm and competence as she battled the pain of a difficult birth. Later, he would do what he could to help her escape the abuse. Gently, he assessed the baby's position. "Your baby is in the breech position."

"That's not good, is it?"

"It's not usually a problem if the mother has access to the facilities of a modern hospital."

"Jeb's mother had her children out here and died trying to deliver her last baby at home." Donna caught her lower lip between her teeth. Fear and desperation were clear in her expression. "I'll die out here too, won't I?"

"Not if I have anything to do with it. I'd like to transfer you to hospital for your own safety. Do you want that, Donna?" The bruises over her body demanded he remove her from the reach of her husband and inform the police.

"He won't let me go." Donna's eyes reddened and she blinked as tears fell down her flushed cheeks.

"I'll inform him that it's necessary for your safety, and that of your baby." In a softer voice, Dan continued. "The hospital social worker can help you leave if you wish to. Think about it."

Two sets of footsteps approached the room. Dan drew a sheet over Donna's lower body and stood beside her.

"Doc?" Greg's voice called before he appeared in the doorway, hands raised like a police suspect.

"What the—?" Dan's question was lost beneath his patient's cry.

"Jeb, no. Don't do this. Please." Donna's plea made no sense until her husband stepped into view, a rifle aimed at Greg's back.

Jeb fixed his gaze on his wife. "She's not going anywhere. You help her birth the baby here and you can be on your way. Without her."

Dan looked at the gun across the width of the room. Was it loaded or just to make a point? Macho bullshit and violence to his wife aside, Dan wondered if Jeb might be struggling with a mental illness. Highly strung patients could be unpredictable at best. And at worst—?

Dan moistened his lips and decided to try calm logic. "Jebediah, the baby is in the wrong position. If we don't get your wife to hospital, you may lose both of them."

"You're a doctor. All your fancy education has got to be some use, else why'd you do all that study? No, you help my Donna with the baby. She'll be fine."

"She needs a Caesarean section. In hospital and—"

Jeb cocked his rifle. The click was loud in the hot afternoon. "And I told you—she's not going to leave me."

Sweat trickled down Dan's back and into his eyes but he didn't dare make any sudden moves. Slowly he raised his hands to chest height, palms facing the gun, and maintained eye contact with Jeb. "Okay, Jeb. But I'm going to need to be patched through to the maternity section of the hospital in Mt. Isa. I haven't delivered a breech baby and I need an obstetrics specialist on hand to guide me.

Can you do that for me? Set up the radio so I can communicate directly with the specialist?"

Donna screamed as another contraction gripped her. Beneath the pink flush of effort, her cheeks were pale.

"Pant, Donna, pant, don't push." As Dan checked her progress, he reviewed what he'd managed to read on breech births so far. Was his theory going to be enough to help Donna?

Chapter Seven

"I'll be there in ten minutes. Have Jessie's Girl ready for me, will you, Johnno?" Amy tapped the end call button and turned to her father. "Something's wrong. Dan and Greg landed well before midday on a routine pickup. Base hasn't heard from them since Greg's call that there was a disagreement between husband and wife about her leaving the property. I'm going to overfly their route and see if I can locate them."

"Where were they headed?" A frown added more wrinkles to her father's forehead.

"Jeb and Donna Campbell's property. I don't know much about them."

"I do. Come on, I'll tell you on the way to the airport." He slapped his hat on his head and strode out the door.

Amy grabbed her car keys and followed. As soon as she had reversed into the street and merged with the afternoon traffic, she glanced at her father. His jaw looked as hard as the granite rocks at the lookout. "Okay, Dad, spill."

"If Jeb is as bad as his father, that young woman is in a pack of trouble. Old man Campbell was a nasty piece of work, mean as they come. Abused his wife and kids, but out on the property, no one was around to see how bad it got. They had seven children and Patty, his wife, died in childbirth with the eighth because he wouldn't allow her to come into town for the birth. All but one, Jeb, left the property and they've never gone back."

"Is the father still alive?" Amy eased back on her speed and her grip on the wheel. It wouldn't help Dan and Greg—or that poor, young, expectant woman—if Amy had an accident on her way to find them. Shoving graphic images of plane wrecks from her mind, she changed lanes and took the turnoff to the airport.

"He died a few years back. Broke his neck falling off the water tank, so the story goes. Jeb inherited the property and took his bride—Donna Tait, she was—out there. Rarely seen them since the wedding, and not at all since she's been pregnant."

"Are they just anti-social?"

"Sweetheart, some families just seem jinxed. The Campbells have had more than their share of abusive men. And maybe because they are never in town, the sons continue the behaviour of their sires. I'd be plenty worried about young Donna right now."

Amy pulled into the parking area and leaned across, hugging her father. "Thanks for being you, Dad. Take my car and go visit Jeff. Tell him I'll call in later tonight but I've got to fly—literally." With a quick kiss on his cheek, she opened her door and raced to the hangar.

Johnno appeared from the rear of the plane as she reached Jessie's Girl. He patted the side panel. "She's good to go, Ames."

"Thanks. Any news since—?"

"Nothing. Look, there isn't anyone free to go up with you so—"

"Yes, there is. Me." Lizzy of the impressive décolletage had pulled on a pair of coveralls and swapped her stilettos for sneakers. "A second pair of eyes might make a difference. I've cleared it with my supervisor. So—am I an acceptable co-searcher?"

Truth to tell, Amy was less than thrilled at the thought of time spent in Lizzy's company. Too self-confident and pushy when it came to men, Lizzy wouldn't be her first choice. She glanced at Johnno who seemed less bemused than she was. What did he know that she didn't?

Johnno wiped his hands on a rag and tucked it into his pocket. A glint of what appeared to be humour shone in his eyes.

Amy looked back at Lizzy.

"I'm in the SES, if that helps. I do know one end of a set of binoculars from the other." The blonde raised her chin and stood her ground, her gaze unwavering on Amy's.

"Sure. Thanks. Climb aboard." What the hell, maybe there was more than a man-eater to Tizzy Lizzy after all.

As soon as they were airborne, Amy handed over the route map Johnno had given her. "Can you read a map, Lizzy?"

"Fair question. Yes. I can also drive an SES truck and I'm learning search and rescue techniques in Johnno's class." Lizzy took the map and studied it. "My job is to read the coordinates out regularly and keep an eye out the window, right?"

"Right."

"Stay on your current course. I'll tell you when X marks the spot."

Amy tipped her head and struggled not to stare at her companion. Tizzy Lizzy had cracked a joke. And, by her own choice, Amy's nemesis and thorn in her side was now her companion on a search and rescue.

"What's the matter, Amy? I'm not always a total bitch." Lizzy raised an eyebrow but her usual tart tone was absent. "Scratch that. I am."

"Sorry, I've just never seen this side of you."

"Yeah, well, I do what I have to so people don't think they can walk all over me."

Gruff and no-nonsense, Lizzy's usual sultry vixen voice had vanished along with her high heels. Feeling like Alice down the rabbit hole, Amy felt her way through a conversation she'd never imagined having. "You're the last person I would expect that to be a problem for."

"There, you see? People don't mess with me. Bear five degrees left, um, is that port? Sorry, I have a problem with left and right."

"It's port. Think that port and left both have four letters and end in 'T'. On second thoughts, scratch the last part. So does right. But the four letters in each word is a handy memory device." Amy descended as low as she could before trying again to raise Greg on his radio.

After that, aside from Lizzy's regular course check, silence reigned in the cockpit. Tension radiated from the right seat in palpable waves, growing more intense the nearer they flew to Dan's pickup location. Was it possible that Lizzy actually had a thing for Dan? Was that why she'd volunteered to come, and why she was tense as a bowstring now? Pity for her co-worker was the last thing Amy expected to feel. But then, she had the advantage of knowing why Dan would never be interested in Lizzy.

"We'll find them. It's probably something trivial like the radio's stopped working or the patient might even be delivering early and they've decided to help her have the baby at home." At least, Amy hoped it was that simple. The closer they came to the homestead without seeing evidence of a crash, the more upbeat she became.

"They were called to the Campbell homestead, weren't they? With the Campbells, it's never simple."

"My father told me a bit about the family as we drove into work."

"That they've a history of the men abusing the women? Yeah, they do." Clipped tones before Lizzy turned her back and scanned through her window discouraged further probing. "There! I can see their plane on the landing strip. It's maybe a kilometre from the house."

Amy radioed base. "We've spotted the plane. It appears undamaged and parked normally at the end of the strip. No success raising Dan or Greg via radio though. We're going to land and walk to the house."

The strip was rough but easier and flatter than the landing to pick up Jeff from a remote corner of their home.

As she pulled up beside the other RFDS plane, Amy began a visual check, which she continued once on the ground. She completed her circuit, patted the plane and walked over to join Lizzy. "The good news is there doesn't appear to be any damage to the plane."

"That may be the only good news. Come on, the homestead's this way." Lizzy marched off with a certainty that confused Amy.

"How do you know it's this way?"

"I checked the area as we flew in and read the map while you were checking the plane." She broke into a jog that revealed a level of fitness Amy had to work to match.

Five minutes later, the homestead came into view through a stand of small trees. Amy's calf muscles protested with the ache of not having warmed up before their run, and she slowed to a walk. Farm dogs barked as they approached, and one hurled itself against the high fence that separated it from the women and the house.

"I'm glad they don't let their dogs roam in the home yard." A shiver ran down Amy's spine as she gave the dogs a wide berth.

Lizzy glanced at her, and one eyebrow rose. "You don't like dogs? I thought you grew up on a property?"

"I was bitten by one when I was a kid. Let's say I have a healthy respect for them and keep my distance now." She opened the gate to the house yard and entered.

Lizzy stopped with her hand on the rusted iron. Her eyes narrowed as she stood at the entrance to the homestead. "I'll take a look around the back."

"Okay." Amy mounted the stairs, calling out as she reached the veranda. "Hello. Anybody home?"

"Come in." The unfamiliar voice sounded tense and Amy wondered whether the gossip had got the situation wrong. It wouldn't be the first time.

"Mr Campbell?" Amy opened the screen door and stepped into a dim, slightly cooler interior. After the bright sunlight, she could just make out the figure of a man as her eyes adjusted to the dark hallway. From a room on her left, a woman cried out. Instinctively, Amy moved to the doorway.

On the bed amid rumpled and blood-streaked sheets, a young woman strained in the throes of what appeared to be a difficult labour. Dan was bent over the woman; her lower half lay exposed. In the opposite corner, Greg sat like a prisoner with his hands behind his neck, and a pinched and pale face.

Before Amy could voice her concern at Greg's unorthodox presence, the strange man stepped in behind her and prodded her in the back with something cold, hard and metallic. "Go and sit beside flyboy over there. Hands on your head where I can see them."

"Do as Jeb says, Captain." Dan's voice was neutral, but he held her gaze and frowned.

As she slid to the floor with her back against a wardrobe, Amy flicked a look at their captor. Aside from the gun he cradled in his arms, he seemed—normal. But what would he do if Lizzy knocked on the back door? Or worse, if she strolled in unannounced? Amy's breath caught on a gasp. He might shoot first and worry about the 'who' later. She couldn't allow that to happen. Mind racing, she scrabbled to find a way to communicate information so Jeb didn't cotton on.

"How's she doing, Dan? Anything I can help with?" Dan was intent on his patient and the woman—Donna, she reminded herself—didn't look good, even to her untrained eye.

"The doc can manage, girly. You just shut your mouth." Jeb leaned against the doorjamb, relaxed with the power balance in his favour.

How could Amy change it? "It's just that the doctor looks like he needs a hand. He's never done a birth like this before."

"A breech birth, you mean?" Jeb's focus flicked between Amy and Dan.

"Under duress. Don't you think the doctor would be able to focus better if you didn't point that gun at him and your wife?"

"Shut up, you stupid little—"

"Jeb, I need another pair of hands. You can put down your gun and help your wife, or let Amy come and help me."

Beneath Dan's calm request, Amy sensed an underlying strain. Slowly, she pushed up until she stood, hands behind her neck. "Jeb? Can I go and help the doctor?"

Jeb's neck muscles corded and his eyes narrowed, his gaze the only thing that moved. Back and forth between Dan and Amy until she wanted to scream in frustration. Finally, he waved her over with the gun. "No talking. Keep your hands where I can see them."

Donna groaned and writhed and her crumpled dress slipped off her swollen stomach as Amy stopped beside Dan and looked down.

"Oh my God." Amy pressed a hand to her mouth and reached blindly for Dan's arm. The gossips had only half the story. Bruises, some livid, others fading, patterned the woman's hips, including across her womb.

Dan manoeuvred Amy's unresisting body to stand up beside Donna's head. Only then did she notice the death grip Donna had on Dan's hand. "Donna, let go of my hand. Amy's here. She'll count you through each contraction. Listen to her, okay?"

Amy blinked and moistened her dry lips. What did Dan want her to do? "What? How do I count?"

"Stupid cow." Jeb's comment barely registered.

Dan paid the man no heed as he demonstrated the pace. "When a contraction starts, count a steady beat and hold her hand. Or rather, let her hold yours. A woman in labour has an almighty strong grip."

Softly, Amy leaned close to him and murmured, "I came with someone. She's—"

Pain contorted Donna's face. Her grip tightened and she began to pant. Conscious of Dan's speculative gaze, Amy counted through the contraction. As Donna's death grip eased, Amy turned to Dan. A flicker of movement at the door caught her eye. Another figure stood quietly beside Jeb.

Lizzy! She'd walked right into a trap. How had she missed seeing Jeb's gun? If only she didn't scream or make a sudden move or—

"Hello, Jebediah. Long time, no see." Lizzy's appearance took everyone by surprise, with the exception of Donna who lay back on her pillow and closed her eyes.

Amy bit her lip, scared of what Donna's husband might do.

He looked at Lizzy and his eyebrow rose. "Lizzy, did you come to see your brother, or to meet your nephew?"

"He's your brother?" Amy looked from one to the other. Now they were standing side by side, the family resemblance was easy to pick; so easy, she wondered why she hadn't noticed when she first saw Jeb.

"The baby might be my niece. Pity the poor little thing in this family if it's a girl."

He leaned against the wall and eyed his sister with disdain. "Girls aren't any use 'cept to ease a man's needs."

"When I was taken away by Children's Services after Mum died, I was told I'd never set foot on this place again. They got that one wrong. They also told me I'd be better off not having any contact with my older siblings." Lizzy looked past Jeb's shoulder at his wife lying in a lather of sweat and bloodied sheets. "I think they were right about that and I bet poor little Donna Tait wishes she'd never had any contact with you either."

"You know nothing about your family. You've been brainwashed against us by that piss-weak aunt." Jeb's face contorted with anger but the gun no longer pointed into the room. He stepped into Lizzy's space.

She stood toe-to-toe and thrust her face into his. "I'm glad Mum's sister took me in when Mum died. It was the only good thing to come out of that time. She said that women in this family don't live long if they stay here. Looks like she was right about that too."

"Shut up."

"Look at your wife. She could die in childbirth like our mother if you don't let her go to hospital. Is that what you want? To kill your wife and baby like our father did his?"

Sobs shook Donna's body, unlike the screams torn from her moments earlier. "Please, take me away from here. I don't want to die. My baby—"

"Shush, Donna, it's okay. We're here." Amy patted the sweaty hand clinging to hers as though she was a lifeline.

"I knew it. I knew you were going to leave me first chance you got. But I'm not going to let you, Donna. Your place is here with me." Jeb had moved to the end of the bed, one hand gripping the ironwork frame, the other, white-knuckled held his gun at his side.

Dan spoke for the first time in ages. "Jeb, we can save both Donna and your baby, but you've got to let us get them to hospital. There isn't much time. Donna's lost quite a lot of blood and she's getting weaker the longer this goes on. Do you want your wife and child to live?"

Lizzy stepped up beside her brother and raised a hand to his shoulder. "Don't be like our father. Trust the doctor and let us take Donna to hospital. Now."

A fly butted against the window, its buzz the only sound as they waited.

"Take her. Get out of here." Jeb turned on his heel and strode away.

"Quickly, in case he changes his mind." Dan yanked the top sheet loose and covered Donna then put an arm under her knees and one behind her back and scooped her off the bed.

Donna flung an arm out and waved at the wardrobe beside Greg. "My suitcase. Please, it's in the wardrobe."

Greg yanked the door open and pulled out a small emerald-green carry-on case. "This one?"

"Yes. Thanks." Lifting her arms around Dan's neck, she rested her head on his shoulder as he carried her through the doorway.

Amy threw medical gear into his bag and snapped it shut and followed. Lizzy held the screen door wide as Dan led the way to Jeb's four-wheel drive before she raced ahead to open the back door.

"I'll drive." Greg's pallor had eased and he climbed into the driver's seat. Amy cradled Donna's head in her lap as Dan joined her in the back, and Lizzy sat up front with Greg.

"Let's go." Dan's command set them moving.

Chapter Eight

"All set back here." Dan buckled his seatbelt for take-off and smiled at his patient. "You will be fine, Donna. I'm sorry if I frightened you but the exaggeration and his sister's pleas worked on Jeb."

"So I'm not going to die, even though right now I feel like death warmed up?" Donna gave him a wan smile but pain glazed her eyes.

"Not even close. As soon as we're airborne I'm going to give you something for the pain and I want you to keep panting like before, even though the desire to push feels really strong."

Lizzy held her sister-in-law's hand. "I'll count with you like Amy did. And when we get to the hospital, I'll let Auntie Trisha know, then I'll get some clothes for you and my new niece or nephew. By the way, nice to meet you, finally."

Jessie's Girl rolled down the strip, gathering speed until the rumble beneath the wheels disappeared and they climbed into the late afternoon sky. Dan released the breath he hadn't realised he'd been holding as they bumped over the track between the homestead and the plane, half expecting to see Jeb in pursuit. It wouldn't have surprised him if the man changed his mind and chased them, intent on taking his wife back.

"Will Greg be okay flying by himself?" Dan knew Amy wasn't convinced her co-pilot was ready for his captain's bars although the outbound flight had been smooth. He swabbed Donna's arm and gave her an injection to ease her pain.

Amy chuckled and he could imagine the impish grin as she replied. "He's a big boy and he's following Tweety Bird home. Apart from the trauma of witnessing a woman in labour, he'll be fine."

Lizzy's gaze connected with his over Donna's stomach. "It might make him grow up from an infuriating, cocksure boy into a half-decent man."

"True. Seeing a woman endure what Donna has makes a man respectful of a woman's strength and total awesomeness." He dealt with the used syringe and checked Donna's pulse and the baby's heartbeat.

Lizzy held Donna's hand and wiped her brow as she panted through a contraction. The two women may not have known one another before but they were being drawn together when it mattered most.

Dan frowned as he slipped into the right hand seat in the cockpit. "How long before we touchdown?"

Amy checked her controls before flipping her wrist up to check her watch. "About thirty minutes. I can give you a little more speed if I climb but I figured our patient might find it less comfortable."

"No, you're right. It's easier for Donna if we stay at a lower altitude." He glanced out the window. Vibrant splashes of colour patterned the rich red earth. An ancient landscape, unchanged since the Dreamtime, it stretched as far as the eye could see. So much to explore, so much he wanted to do.

He looked sideways at Amy. Kissing her again was his new number one goal. And, for an agonising time today, he'd wondered if he'd live to learn the real sweetness of her mouth. A new life and the chance to follow his dream in the west was his for the taking. Gosford would not hold him back.

"Look, I know you'll want to visit your brother tonight but—do you want to grab a bite to eat after that?"

"Sounds good. How about you join Dad and me and we'll share a bottle of wine? I reckon we've earned it. Ask Greg, and Lizzy too, although I suspect she'll want to stay with Donna and get to know her sister-in-law and the baby. How does Chinese takeaway sound?"

"Fine. Great." Except it wasn't quite what he'd meant, but it was probably for the best. "I'll go and ask Lizzy now."

##

Amy brushed grit from the corner of her eye, thankful she'd had only a single glass of wine last night. Being a pilot meant she was a lightweight drinker, or else after the incident at the Campbell property, she'd probably have missed work today.

"Where's Lizzy this morning?" Amy leaned on the office counter as Tess sorted through the pile of letters in front of her.

Tess looked up and frowned. "I don't know. Probably sick. She was weird when the call came in about Dan and Greg yesterday. And when she bolted out of here, I thought she was having some sort of fit. I mean, she threw her Jimmy Choos into the corner. Jimmy Choos! Who does that kind of shit?"

"Hmm." If Lizzy hadn't revealed details of her family connection with their patient, Amy wasn't going to say anything. "Do you know if Dan is at work yet?"

"He hasn't been in here. Hang on—" Tess looked past Amy's shoulder and waved madly.

The office door opened and tingles of awareness ran down Amy's spine.

Tess grinned broadly at the newcomer. "Hey, Dan, Amy was looking for you"—Tess smirked like a fourteen-year-old in the playground— "Amy, Dan's here."

"Thanks, Tess. Dan, got a minute?" Without pausing for his answer, she led the way into the hangar and didn't stop until she'd put several planes between her and prying eyes.

"Everything okay?" he asked and leaned against Jessie's Girl.

"Yes. Have you heard how Donna is?"

"Her baby boy was born early this morning by C-section. Mother, baby, and aunt are doing well." Shadows underscored Dan's eyes and he seemed a little less . . . standoffish. His gaze roamed her face with an intensity she hadn't seen before. It unnerved her, and it excited her.

"Wonderful. Good news."

"Was there something else on your mind?" It looked like he had plenty on his.

"Do you have to make a report about—sorry, that's none of my business. Lizzy's family is her business, not mine or theirs." She jerked a thumb in the direction of the office.

Dan glanced towards the office and shook his head. "I'm not sure what you're talking about."

"Tess didn't seem to know Lizzy flew out with me yesterday, or that she stayed at the hospital with Donna. I figured it was better not to mention it in case Lizzy doesn't want her association with Jeb known. Heaven knows, I wouldn't want to belong to the same family."

"Good idea. If I recall, her surname is Wilmot. Seems she took her aunt's name when she went to live with her."

Amy threaded her fingers together and pressed her hands over her tummy. Why couldn't she simply say the words to invite Dan out? He'd said they were friends and friends did things. Like having a drink together. "Will you go back to see Donna tonight? I thought I'd pop in before I visit Jeff, and maybe get to hold the baby."

"Probably. Look, I'm on my way to see the boss now. Can we have dinner on Saturday? After rehearsals? I want to ask you something."

Dinner? As though he'd read her mind, the invitation tantalised and hung, shimmering in the air between them. She knew nothing could come of it, given Dan's preference for men, but they could be friends, couldn't they? And friendship with Dan would be a step in the right direction, a beginning to healing after Derek's perfidy.

"Congratulations, Donna. He's a handsome little fellow." As 'Baby' Campbell lay in Amy's arms, he found his thumb, closed his eyes, and started sucking. She leaned close and inhaled his sweet baby scent. "Any thoughts on his name?"

Lizzy walked in and closed the door behind her. "I can guarantee one name that's not a contender. Is it my turn to hold him yet?"

Their shared experience seemed to have brought a truce that Amy hoped would last. Lizzy was a strong woman of unsuspected depths, far removed from the bimbo image Amy had failed to see beyond. The Tizzy Lizzy nickname would never pass her lips again. Amy grinned and handed Lizzy's nephew over. "What names do you like, Lizzy?"

"David, Michael, Harrison . . . I don't know. Donna?"

Donna eased herself higher up her pillows, grimacing with the movement. "My stitches pull when I move. What do you think of Dan? Do you think Doctor Dan would mind?"

"I bet he'll be honoured." Crooning to her nephew, Lizzy gently rocked him as she strolled to the window. "Who's the most handsome young man in all the world? Dan, Danny boy, Dan the man . . . it's the perfect name for you."

"Knock, knock, can a male come in?" Dan popped his head around the door before entering. Barely concealed behind his back, he carried a bunch of flowers and a purple teddy bear. A blue helium balloon with 'Welcome, baby boy' in a curly, fancy font, floated above his head.

"Dan, thanks for visiting again. Your timing is perfect." Donna looked at Lizzy and Amy, and raised her eyebrows. Both nodded, and she turned back to Dan.

"I'm intrigued. What can I do for you?" He put the flowers on the bedside table and sat on the chair beside her bed.

"I'd like to name my baby after you, if you don't mind?"

Dan lowered his head and fiddled with the purple satin bow on the teddy's neck. For one awful moment, Amy thought he was going to refuse. How could he? Why would he? But when he looked up at Donna, his smile stretched from ear to ear. He set the bear on the cover and took her hand between both of his. "I'm honoured. It's a wonderful gift you've given me. Thank you."

Lizzy brought young Dan over and placed him in Dan's arms. "Say hello to your namesake. Eighteen-hours-old and already a heart-breaker."

Dan nursed the baby with an ease and tenderness that brought a lump to Amy's throat. He should have children of his own. He'd be a wonderful father. Pressing one hand to her stomach, she headed towards the door. "I'd better get a move on and visit Jeff. He'll want to hear why I've abandoned him the last couple of days. Donna, I'll visit again tomorrow. Bye, Lizzy, Dan." Her gaze lingered on him as she pulled the door closed behind her.

In the corridor, she leaned against the wall and let her head fall back as she stared into a fluorescent light. The image of Dan holding the baby was burned into her mind. Try as she may, she couldn't convince herself that he was a man who would be content not to have children of his own.

Chapter Nine

"Ladies, you come in on the first count of the fifth bar. Mike, you're holding your ukulele like a bass guitarist. Lift it higher." Dan jumped off the stage of the community hall and strode to his sound system, and reset the music to the opening notes of the intro. "Okay, let's try that again. And-a-one, two, three-and—"

In the front row of metal chairs, Amy chewed her bottom lip in frustration.

Dan shared the feeling, although he was pretty sure their reasons were different. She'd worked hard writing the script for Terri's luau performance; the bones of the show were good, even if the performers were under-rehearsed and unable to count past four.

But each time her teeth captured her full lower lip, he wanted to pull her into his arms and kiss her. Just one proper kiss—okay, stopping at one was never going to happen.

Footsteps tapped across the wooden floor in time with the music and stopped beside him.

"How's it going?" Lizzy dumped a large tote bag on the nearest chair and folded her arms. "Hmm, looks like they need some help."

Amy jumped up and joined them. "Lizzy, how's Donna and young master Dan?"

"Great. My aunt can't believe her luck. She adores babies and she's fussing over Donna as if she was her own daughter. It's good for all of them."

"You could have brought them over for a look. Although we're—" Amy's glance at the stage was eloquent.

"Struggling? I thought I'd come join you and get out of their hair for the evening. Looks like I got here just in time."

Dan stopped the music. "Glad to have you on board. Hop up there and see if you can get the hula girls to come in at the start of the fifth bar."

Lizzy grinned and kicked off her sandals and bounded up the stairs to the stage. "Can't count to save themselves I reckon, doc. Come on, you lot. Let's nail this and then we can go to the pub."

The hour's practice sailed by and Dan called time. "Well done, everyone. Thanks. Amy, any last comments?"

"Aside from a huge thank you to all of you, that's it. Full dress rehearsal next Friday night. Any costume issues—"

"See me." Mouths agape, the women stared at Lizzy.

"What? I've got taste, style and a sewing machine courtesy of my aunt. Besides, Amy's got more than enough on her plate. She doesn't need anyone whining about itchy coconut bras." Unconcerned by the looks thrown her way, Lizzy sat and strapped on her fashion sandals. The others drifted to the side benches and collected their gear.

Dan chuckled and turned to pack up his sound system. Lizzy sure knew how to take charge and get action. And how to throw her co-workers for a loop. It seemed she had decided Amy was okay and thrown her support behind her.

Amy appeared at his side, her laptop clutched in one hand and a gym bag in the other. "That was a really good rehearsal, especially once Lizzy got here. I didn't know she had such a good sense of rhythm and timing, and she moves so well."

"You wrote a great scene, Amy. It will be a hit on the night."

"Thanks. You—didn't mention where we're going for dinner. I, um, brought a good dress to change into, in case it was somewhere that, you know, needed—"

"Who's up for the pub? Amy? Dan?" Tess bounced up to them, a bright smile replacing her usual little sneer.

Lizzy stood and linked arms with Tess. "You know, you haven't told me about that cute guy you said you wanted to go out with. Come and tell me all about him." She turned to Amy and Dan was certain she winked as she added, "See you at work on Monday."

"Dan, did what I think happen just happen?"

"Yep, Lizzy's become human."

"Not quite what I expected when you invited me to dinner." Amy inhaled the fragrant aroma of the Thai entrée Dan placed in front of her. Bamboo placemats and apple green linen serviettes graced the table, one of his mother's housewarming gifts when he graduated and moved into his own apartment.

Dan served himself and slid into the seat opposite. He flicked open his serviette and dropped it across his trousers. "I had to answer the challenge you laid down."

"What challenge?"

"My first day on the job, at the pub. You reckoned I couldn't cook. I thought I should show you I'm not just a pretty face. Tuck in."

Amy tasted her Pho Ga soup and glanced at Dan. "It's delicious. Did you really make this yourself?"

"I'm wounded to the core that you doubt me. And so would my mother be. Check out the rubbish bin if you like. You won't find any takeaway containers lurking in the depths." Sending silent thanks to his mother for teaching him how to cook in his teens, he dipped his spoon into his bowl.

"Tell me about your mother. She's a doctor too, isn't she?"

"Both Mum and my grandfather, although he retired a few years ago. Mum used to take me along to her bush clinics when I was little. I remember being fascinated by the places we visited and later, by the range of work Mum did in remote communities. It seemed she helped so many people and I wanted to be like her and Gramps."

"Where did your grandfather work?"

"He was a Flying Doctor for many years in New South Wales."

"And now you're continuing the family tradition. That's wonderful, Dan."

"It's been my goal since I began studying medicine. I figured I'd get a specialty and some experience in a big hospital before I took to the air. It—happened sooner than I'd planned." He scooped up the rest of his soup and cleared the empty bowls. As much as he wanted to clear the air with Amy, telling her about Gosford seemed more than he was ready for.

Clattering the dishes in the sink, he served the next course, taking more time than necessary to add the coriander and chilli curl garnish. "I hope you like chilli? I should have asked before today."

"Love it. What have you cooked?"

"One of my favourites. Green curry chicken with eggplant and corn." He set one dish in each place and turned back to collect a communal bowl of rice, which he placed close to Amy.

"Oh my God, that smells awesome."

"Please start." Dan watched as Amy helped herself to the main course before serving himself, but his appetite had deserted him. A mouthful of wine didn't help, not when his stomach was turning cartwheels. The evening would end up a disaster if he didn't pull himself together. Amy was already watching him as though she wasn't sure whether to call the men in white coats.

Psyching himself up, he put down his fork and met Amy's enquiring gaze. "I said I had something to ask you but I'm finding it hard to know where to start."

She put her fork down and picked up her wine glass. "The beginning is usually a good place."

"Something happened in Gosford and I felt I had to leave. Start afresh. The vacancy up here hadn't even been advertised but I heard about it through a friend who works for the RFDS in New South Wales. I applied and here I am." He drank a mouthful of wine and reached for the bottle to top up their glasses.

"O . . .kay. So . . . what did you want to ask me?"

What did he want from her? Since the incident at the Campbell property, a strong compulsion to get to know Amy better had gripped him. But he couldn't begin any sort of relationship until he'd cleared the air. She deserved to know the skeleton in his closet and decide for herself what sort of man he was.

"How much had you heard about—me before I started?"

"Not a thing other than your name. Why?"

"The night we met, I thought you must have heard about what happened in Gosford."

"I didn't even know who you were then. Other than the bloke who'd laughed when he saw my knickers and whose beer I'd tipped over him." Her smile encouraged him to continue.

"The beer missed my shirt. But Mike told me who you were and I assumed you knew who I was. When you stopped to help me at the side of the road, I thought you were angry to be partnered with me."

"I was embarrassed because I'd behaved childishly when you laughed at me."

"Not at you. Like any red-blooded male, I was appreciating the view." And hadn't that normal masculine reaction blown out of proportion in his mind, all because of one incident? Certain that his new pilot knew of the allegation against him, he had subdued the natural attraction he'd felt for Amy and fought to remain neutral in their daily interactions.

"Dan, what did happen in Gosford?"

His stomach clenched as fear tightened his throat. Leaving Gosford had been about leaving behind the allegations and now, he was about to bring the past crashing into his present. But wasn't this why he'd asked Amy to dinner?

Fighting the attraction had proven to be harder than he'd foreseen. And facing the business end of a gun had reminded him how tenuous life could be. He didn't want to give up the chance that Amy might just like him for himself. That she might believe in him.

"A young intern, a woman, had begun stalking me. One night, she abandoned her post in Emergency and threw herself at me. I was trying to extricate myself without causing a fuss when the head doctor, her uncle, walked in. She spotted him before I knew he was standing behind me. She'd already been in a bit of strife over her substandard performance; leaving Emergency when she did would have been the end of her career so she accused me of sexually harassing her."

Amy reached across the table and covered his hand. "What an awful thing to happen to you. Is that what you meant when you asked if I knew about you?"

"Yes. I've always tried to create a pleasant and happy workplace. Maybe I gave her the wrong idea and she thought I was—interested—if you know what I mean?" Each time he'd examined his working relationship with Carissa, the conclusion was the same. He'd treated her the same as all the other interns in the hospital.

"What happened then?"

"Colleagues stood up and openly offered their support, but I felt like everyone was—wondering. No smoke without fire, you know?" Thankful he'd had good working relationships with people who were prepared to defend him had helped him get through the inquiry. But the slur cast over his good name had bit deep.

"Anyone who knows you wouldn't think that. But what I don't understand is why this—intern thought you'd be interested in her, anyway?" Amy rested her elbows on the table and lowered her chin onto her folded hands as she posed the question. Wrangling with that had kept him awake nights too.

"She was attractive and knew it. And I've always been friendly and encouraging to my staff. Maybe she misread that as more than it was."

"Is that why you've been distant with the women at work? Well, with the single ones, at least?"

"Was it that obvious?"

"Duh, yeah. You even had me wondering if you were a misogynistic b—"

"No, I'm not. But I don't want to go through anything like that again." It seemed caution had made him standoffish and he wanted to rectify that.

"Dan, you're a good-looking man and women will always appreciate looking. That doesn't mean every female is out to make life difficult for you."

"You make me sound like a pompous ass. I'm just being careful."

"So careful you've become a challenge to half the females on base!" Amy shook her head and picked up her fork. With a pile of noodles halfway to her mouth, she paused and looked at him with a speculative gleam in her eyes. "You could tell them, you know. Like you did with me."

Shuddering at the thought, Dan wound thin noodles onto his fork and forced himself to eat a mouthful. "Telling you was hard enough. No, I just want a comfortable workplace with no complications."

"Dan, so far, you've told me why you joined the RFDS, but you haven't asked me anything. What do you want me to do?"

"I want to make it clear I'm not 'available'."

"How will you do that?"

"By giving everyone a clear message that I'm not—available."

"How do you plan to do that?"

"Will you be my girlfriend?"

Chapter Ten

"So, you and Doctor Dan are going out, hey, Amy?"

"What?" Amy gripped her clipboard and turned to see Sharyn leaning nonchalantly against the door from the office. Narrowed eyes pinned her to the spot and Sharyn's stretched lips barely passed as a facsimile of a smile.

If word was already out about Amy and Dan dating, the gossip mill had beaten all previous records. Amy clasped the clipboard to her chest. Dan had agreed not to say anything and she trusted his word. So how—?

"You really should be more careful if you want to keep your— relationship—a secret. But he's such a hottie, why would you?"

"We're not. I mean, what makes you think we are?"

"Oh, that neat little side step after rehearsal for one thing. Tess told me you avoided going to the pub with the rest of the cast, and so did dishy Doctor Dan."

"We had a—planning dinner. People have working meals all the time."

Sharyn grinned as though she'd won first prize.

Mentally, Amy kicked herself. Avoiding Sharyn's fishing tactic should have been a no-brainer but now she'd handed confirmation and details to a woman who would use them to gain whatever leverage she could.

"Is that what you're calling it?" Sharyn held out her right hand and paid her manicure an undue amount of attention. "Looked more like mouth-to-mouth resuscitation to me."

Heat blazed through Amy as she recalled that one simple kiss on the cheek as she left Dan's house. He'd held her shoulders and bent close enough that his aftershave was imprinted on her senses. Close enough that she'd been tempted to turn her head and connect with his mouth in a way that would have satisfied her curiosity about Doctor Dan. In a way that wouldn't have been fair to Dan's preferences or to the trust he'd shown in asking for her help.

So she'd resisted the temptation and accepted his chaste kiss on her cheek. Ironically, the kiss, brief and chaste as it was, had been seen and noted as exactly what she wished it could be. As what Amy would have liked it to have been if her world was more giving.

"Don't make out on the front veranda if you don't want to kiss and tell. Oh, and here's a tip for you, Tweety Bird. A bloke like the doc, he won't stick around for long with a woman like you. He needs someone more—" Her eyes narrowed on something past Amy's shoulder. "Hi, Dan, I heard it was a good rehearsal. Sorry I couldn't make it. I was just telling Amy that you need someone more experienced to whip those girls into shape."

Dan came to a halt beside Amy and met her gaze before answering Sharyn. "Lizzy was great. She got them to dance in time and energised them, didn't she, Amy?"

"Yeah, she was tops." For the life of her, Amy couldn't come up with anything more. Should she let Dan know that their 'secret' was common knowledge already?

Sharyn pushed off the wall and drew level with Dan. One finger traced a path across his chest before she stepped in close to him. "I'm having a small party at my place next weekend. You'll come, won't you, Dan? It won't be any fun if you don't." She offered a pretty pout and a flutter of her false eyelashes.

Dan tensed and eased away. Towards Amy.

Understanding what he needed, Amy slipped her hand into his and pressed up against his side. "I'm not sure if we're free but we'll let you know. Thanks for asking us, Sharyn."

Amy looked up at Dan, hoping like crazy she'd done what he wanted.

He smiled at her, and nodded before turning to Sharyn. "Yes, thanks for the invitation. Can we let you know later?"

Venom filled Sharyn's eyes as her gaze connected with Amy's and, just for a moment, Amy was reminded of the taipan she'd seen up close on a long-ago school excursion.

"No worries, Dan. And, hey, good to see you're—making friends. Toodles."

As soon as the door closed behind Sharyn, Dan squeezed Amy's hand. "Did she really just say 'toodles'?"

Amy nodded and bit her lip before laughter burst forth. "Oh my God, have you been putting up with—that—since you arrived?"

"Yep. See why I needed a bad-ass pilot to protect me? Thanks for throwing yourself into the fray."

Amy sobered immediately and looked around. Nobody was nearby but she lowered her voice. "She knew already. About us. She saw us on your veranda. It sounds like she's stalking you. I didn't think to ask how she came to be outside your house last night."

"Sharyn was at my home last night?"

"Maybe she happened to be driving by. But yeah, she saw us and felt compelled to track me down to tell me. Tess spilled the beans about us not joining the after-rehearsal drinks."

"Amy, I'm sorry if I've put you in a difficult situation. When I asked you to be my girlfriend, I promised to give you time to consider."

"Looks like you're stuck with me for now. So, boyfriend, I'll expect a Thai meal like that every week to keep me sweet." She winked at Dan, turned, and took three steps away, then turned back and fluttered her fingers. "Toodles, darling."

##

Dan watched Amy disappear around the rear of the plane and a feeling of light-hearted relief suffused him. She knew about Gosford and she trusted him. He could work with that. He straightened his shoulders and headed for the office.

"So, Doc, you and our Tweety Bird, hey? Didn't see that coming." Johnno tossed a spanner in a couple of passes between his hands.

"It's recent."

"None of my business. So long as she's happy, it'll stay that way."

"Understood. But I don't intend to hurt her." Ridiculously, it made Dan feel good knowing others were watching out for Amy. Especially if Sharyn decided to make life difficult.

Amy was strong minded and independent but he didn't want to cause problems for her. Pretending to be his girlfriend would surprise some colleagues and stop the less than subtle efforts of some of the women. From their pretence, he would build their relationship into the real thing.

Strangely, facing a gun had given him clarity and perspective. What had been a giant thundercloud hanging over his head was now no more than a petty annoyance that would fade in time.

"We had dinner after rehearsals last night and decided to—give it a go."

"So I heard. Tess made sure everybody knew." Johnno cracked a wry grin. "Why don't you and Ames come over for drinks on Wednesday. Terri won't want to miss out on the story of how you two met while working on her show."

"I'll check with Amy. Her brother may be released from hospital mid-week. We'll know more tomorrow."

"Fair enough." Johnno turned back to the engine part on the bench and the sound of metal on metal clanged through the workshop.

Dan continued to the office and a pile of paperwork. Digital or physical, some aspects of work never changed.

##

"Are you really busy? Can I have a word, Dan?" Amy poked her head around his office door.

Dan flexed his fingers and leaned back in his chair. "Come in. It's time I had a break."

"Thanks." Amy perched on the edge of a chair and sat on her hands. She bit her lip and he forgot all about work, and the report required by the police on Jebediah Campbell. There was no room in his body for thoughts of anything other than Amy and her delectable mouth. Why hadn't he sealed their deal with a proper kiss? Finally, the tension radiating from her registered with him and he sought her gaze.

"Is everything okay?"

"Yes. No. Probably." Her attention wandered to his mouth before flicking back to his eyes. She cleared her throat. "We didn't really think this through very well."

"What are you talking about?" Coherent thought fled as he recalled her soft skin, warm and silky in the tropical night, and the scent of her shampoo as his nose brushed her hair.

"Our—relationship. Couples behave in certain ways—touch one another. Kiss."

"Your point is . . .?"

"Well, you won't exactly want to—kiss me."

"Won't I? Please tell me why you think that might be a problem." If only she knew how much he wanted to kiss her right at this moment. She'd probably run and keep running until she crossed the border. 'Friends', she'd said, and he had to be careful not to scare her away with his desire for more than that. Not yet.

"After what happened to you, and knowing about your—background, I thought—well, why would you want to kiss me?"

"I don't have a problem with kissing you. In fact, I suspect I might—enjoyit."

"You do? But—"

"Here's an idea. Tell me if you don't like it. How about we try one now?"

"Now? Right now?"

"Yes."

"Here, in your office?" Her voice was breathy and she looked around as though expecting to see dozens of people.

He scooted his roller chair close and lightly traced her jaw. "We're alone. What do you think? Shall we see how we go?"

Her eyes widened and her lips parted. Wordlessly, she nodded and leaned towards him.

He kept this first kiss light, brushing her mouth with his, and barely tasting her sweetness. Her lips clung to his and he dared a little more. A gentle nip on her full lower lip that had taunted his dreams. Warm breath shared, she pulled back and looked at him.

Wonder of wonders. Amy touched her mouth and blinked.

Dan's kiss delighted her, both teasing and feeling so real she wanted to dive right back into it. If Dan could kiss her like this, like he meant it, they might just get away with their charade. The only problem she foresaw was wanting more than he could give. She pressed her thighs together and wriggled further back on her seat.

"Well?"

"You'll do." Oh, how he would do!

"Should we practise more? I think we should try standing."

"No need, honestly, Dan."

He seemed a little disappointed. Her reply had been lacklustre, especially given how hard it must be for Dan to kiss a woman. It wasn't his fault he preferred men. Although, that kiss had surpassed her expectations. Blown them away by the promise of more. She took a deep breath and met his gaze.

"That was fine. Really nice."

"Just—nice? I'm sure I can do better. I must be out of practice." He got to his feet and, taking her hand, drew her up.

She rested her hands on Dan's chest, feeling the steady beat of his heart beneath her palm. Hers thudded wildly as she waited, wanting, not wanting, unsure of her reaction if he really kissed her. Properly. Like she wanted him to.

Dan cupped her face with one hand and lowered his head.

"Paging Dr Middleton and Captain Alistair. Please report to your plane. Dr Middleton and Captain Alistair." The tinny voice crackled over the loudspeaker, breaking the spell of Dan's lips.

"We're needed, Dan. I'll—meet you at the plane." She spun on her heel and raced from his office.

Lizzy met her in the corridor outside Dan's door. "Amy, here's the details of the call out."

Amy tucked a loose strand of hair behind her ear and thanked her stars she hadn't been wearing lipstick. Streaked lipstick and messy hair. Telltale signs like that would fuel the rumour mill in ways she and Dan didn't need. "Thanks, Lizzy."

"How's your brother? He must be almost ready to be discharged?" Lizzy walked with her as they headed into the hangar.

"He's making good progress. Maybe Wednesday or Thursday, the hospital said. Dan thinks the same."

"Will you have a welcome home party for him?"

"Maybe."

Lizzy gripped her forearm and, lowering her voice, leaned close. "Watch out for Sharyn. You and the doc, that's got her riled madder than a cut snake. She rather fancied herself snagging him."

Amy looked at the woman who had been the office bitch as long as she'd been there and who now seemed to be a friend. You never knew what lay beneath the face people presented to the world. "Thanks, Lizzy. I'm sure we'll be fine. She's just miffed that he's chasing someone in trousers." Amy hoped no one suspected the truth behind her throwaway line. Not for a while, at least.

"Watch your back." Lizzy headed towards the main office. Through the glass panel, Amy saw her laughing and shaking her head at Tess before the sound of footsteps brought her back to the present.

"Captain, ready to fly?" Dan carried his medical bag in one hand and slipped his iPhone into his shirt pocket with the other.

"Ready, Doc." They climbed aboard and settled into the round of familiar pre-flight checks, the pattern calming Amy's churning thoughts. Later, when they returned, she'd think about Dan's kiss. And about how she was going to manage to keep her head out of the clouds if he kissed her again.

Chapter Eleven

Dan moved around the front of Jeff's wheelchair and pulled on the brakes. "Okay, take it easy and slide your backside across the seat."

On the other side of his car, Amy opened the passenger door and climbed in, arms ready to guide her brother. "Here's your seatbelt, Jeff."

"Yes, mother hen. Don't you think I'm big enough and ugly enough to do it for myself?" Jeff winced as Dan lifted his leg in its plaster cast.

"Hop in, Amy. Let's get this show on the road." Dan held the door as Amy slipped into the front seat. She seemed a bit twitchy and he wondered if it was only because her brother and her parents would be staying with her for a few weeks. Time recuperating at Amy's home before he attempted the long drive back to the family property had been non-negotiable, especially when he needed to access the hospital for physiotherapy.

Dan drove smoothly through the lunchtime traffic, chatting about mundane topics until they pulled into Amy's drive. Gareth and Jessie Alistair came down the front steps to greet them and help Jeff into the house. With one parent on each side, Jeff swung his crutches slowly along the garden path.

Amy grabbed Dan's arm and held him back. Her clear hazel gaze darted from the retreating backs of her family and fixed on him. "Remember, play it down."

"I got it the first time, Amy. We're dating but it's not serious." Even if he wanted it to be, rushing Amy into anything was a sure way to scare her off. "No kissing needed to convince the folks we're together."

"Okay, good, just checking."

He followed her into the house. Jessie Alistair was fussing with Amy's cushions, tucking them behind her son.

"Mum, it's fine there, thanks."

Dan watched the byplay between mother and son, and glanced at Amy. She rolled her eyes and disappeared down the hallway with Jeff's overnight bag. Jeff would need the patience of a saint if his mother didn't find something else to divert her attention from her son.

"I'll make a pot of tea." Jessie went into the kitchen and the sounds of water boiling and pottery mugs being set out filtered into the lounge room.

Dan sat on a footstool beside the television. "So, Jeff, what are your plans to stay occupied while you give your leg time to heal?"

"Go stir crazy probably." Jeff closed his eyes and took a deep breath. "Any suggestions, Doc?"

"How are you at graphic design? We need some stuff done up for the Flying Doctor fundraiser."

"Not my area of expertise. I'm colour blind."

"Lucky you weren't into flying like Amy."

Gareth returned with a box full of folders and a laptop and put them on the table beside his son before sitting in the sleek armchair. "I thought you might like to look over our breeding programme while you've got time to read. See if you can tweak it."

Jeff looked at his father and grinned before reaching across the arm of the chair and grabbing a folder. "Beaut, thanks, Dad. I wondered how I was going to pass my time here."

"You have an interest in genetics? What traits are you looking at?" It had been a close run thing at uni, a toss up between genetics and paediatrics when Dan was choosing his specialty area. His choice had come down to what was the best fit for his ultimate goal of rural medicine.

Jeff pulled out a photo and held it out to Dan. "Drought hardiness, and tick resistance are our primary goals but then we're looking for tender, flavoursome meat. That's one of our successes."

"Export market?"

"Out of Cairns to Asia."

Amy passed through on her way into the kitchen and flicked him a worried look. He smiled in response to her raised eyebrow. All was going well so far.

A few minutes later, she and her mother reappeared with a tray of tea things and a plate of biscuits and homemade fruit cake, which they placed on the coffee table.

Jessie piled up a plate and handed it to her son. "Your favourite, darling. And we're cooking roast beef with all the trimmings for dinner."

Amy placed a mug on the arm of Jeff's chair and carried one across to Dan. He caught her hand and twined his fingers with hers. "When do you want to tell them?"

"Hey, spill. Are you two an item now?" Jeff's question knocked any plans to delay sharing the news until later.

Amy spun around to face her brother and parents. "Look, it's not what it looks like. Well, it is, but it isn't."

Dan tugged her down and she sat on his knee. "Amy and I are going out but it's very new."

Eyes glistening, Jessie clasped her hands together. "Oh, darling, that's wonderful news. Isn't it, Gareth?"

Gareth looked at his son and shrugged. "Er, yeah. Good news."

Jessie hovered with her hand on her husband's shoulder. "Amy, darling, will you help me prepare the vegetables for dinner?"

Amy turned her head and whispered to Dan. "That's mum-code for tell me everything. Please come and rescue me if I'm not out within ten minutes."

"Would you like an emergency at work, or the suggestion we need some alone time?"

The panicked look in Amy's eyes made him relent.

"Work, it is." With her mother looking on fondly, he gave Amy a kiss on her cheek.

"What's that for?"

"Luck." He winked and released her hand.

The warmth of his touch and the humour of his wink carried her through her mother's kitchen inquisition, and the rest of the evening. And when she fell into bed, it was Dan's face and touch that lulled her to sleep.

Without Johnno to keep the younger mechanic in check, her good mood from the previous evening leached away as the day wore on and disappeared completely with Mike's needling over coffee at the afternoon tea break. By the time Dan pulled up outside Terri and Johnno's home, she couldn't hold in her temper any longer.

"Tell me what Johnno said to you." Hands on hips, Amy planted her feet on the yellowing grass footpath outside Johnno and Terri's house. A long day followed by Mike's smirking comment about Johnno and Dan's discussion had fired her temper. "I refuse to go inside until you tell me what he said about me that Mike thought was so funny."

Dan spread his hands, palms up, as he rounded the back of his car. "Johnno just wanted to let me know that there are people looking out for you."

"I can take care of myself. I don't need a man watching me like a hawk. Who does he think he is, warning you off? I've a good mind to—"

Dan covered her hands with his. Startled, she realised she'd made fists of them.

"Amy, he cares about you. Don't make a fuss or you'll embarrass him."

"But—"

"Mike was being a dozy B. You know he likes to stir you. Now can we just go in and have a drink with friends?" The hint of husky voice was so unlike Dan and it occurred to Amy that his start had been even earlier than hers. Sympathy filled her and she nodded.

"If you're sure that was all it was. I hate being gossiped about, especially after—"

A door squeaked and Johnno peered out from the veranda. "Hey, are you two coming in anytime soon? Terri's got kebabs on the barbeque and the beer's getting warm."

"Coming, Johnno." Amy knew she needed to settle down and forget Mike's stupid remark, and enjoy the evening.

Dan took her arm but stopped with a hand on the latch of the front gate. Hooking his arm around her waist he pulled her up close. "Are you okay, Amy? We don't have to stay long if you're tired."

"Dan, I'm sorry. I shouldn't have jumped on you like that. It's just—frustrating having my every move watched. I haven't lived with my family for years and now, I don't seem to have any personal space. Anywhere."

"Okay. If that's all it is, let's try to relax for a couple of hours."

His body was warm and comforting and she told herself to relax like Dan had suggested. She lowered her head onto his shoulder and her nose brushed bare skin in the open neck of his shirt. Breathing in Dan's scent, she closed her eyes. Her hand crept up his chest, sliding over his shirt, feeling the flex of muscles beneath her fingers as he raised his hand.

Dan released her hair from its tie and softly massaged her scalp. Was it her imagination or did his lips touch her head? Amy sighed as the day's tensions drained away.

"We can leave if you like?" Dan's warm breath tickled her ear.

It would be so easy to hop in the car, drive home and snuggle up with Dan for her pillow. Except—her home was full of family who would want to chat about her day and ask how she felt. Beautiful people who loved her and drove her crazy at the same time.

"Terri's made kebabs. We can't disappoint her." Amy inhaled Dan's scent one more time and then, with a supreme effort of will, lifted her head and looked at him. "We'll have to have an evening in at your home again soon."

##

Amy wanted to come back to his home? Either she was more tired than he thought and rambling or . . .

The alternative put a spring in his step as they walked along the garden path.

Terri opened the screen door and grinned as she looked from one to the other. "Hi, guys. Come on through to the pool. Kebabs are ready and I've made a new dipping sauce I want you to try. You're my guinea pigs." They led the way through to the back of the house and Johnno offered a choice of wine or beer when they sat at the table.

"Just water please. I'm half asleep on my feet and I'm flying tomorrow." Amy picked up a carrot stick from the plate of nibbles and dipped it in creamy dip. As she took a bite a smear of sauce coated her lower lip.

Dan's gaze zeroed in on her mouth and he froze, his stubby halfway to his mouth. He could lean across the short distance between them and help her lick it clean. The taste of Amy with—

"Dan, try some of the antipasto." The plate rose in his peripheral vision.

With a start, Dan remembered they weren't alone. "Not for me, thanks." Leaning his arms on the table, he raised his stubby and took a swig. Not that anything would douse the heat pulsing through him. Nothing but losing himself in Amy's body.

Johnno placed a platter of steaming kebabs in the centre of the table and sat next to Amy. Terri added two bowls of dipping sauce, one between each couple, and a bowl of layered salad. "Okay, two, four, six, eight, bog in—"

"Don't wait. It looks and smells wonderful, Terri. Thanks for inviting us." Amy took two skewers and a scoop of salad. "How's the fundraiser planning coming along? Need a hand with anything else?"

"All undercontrol." Terri served herself and picked up her fork.

"She's only pulled her hair out once this week." Johnno hoed into his kebab and grinned when Terri mock-punched his arm.

They reminded Dan of his parents, and his hopes of finding the same kind of relationship one day. Gosford had burned him, it was true. Amy had remarked on his standoffish behaviour with the women on base, but as he watched her with her friends—his friends now, too—the past slipped away. With luck on his side, Amy was his future.

He just had to convince her he was hers.

Johnno refilled their glasses and cleared away the plates before rejoining them. "Coffee's on, unless anyone prefers tea?" With no takers for tea, he sat and linked hands with his wife.

Terri leaned forward. "I'm really pleased you two are together. You're a perfect couple. We both agree."

"Oh, Terri, we're just going out and having a bit of fun. Nothing serious." Amy toyed with her glass of water and glanced at Dan. "Aren't we, Dan?"

"Sure." He raised his stubby and toasted her. Fun was the best way to start his pursuit of Amy. And it looked as if he could count Terri on his side.

Across the table, Johnno's gaze connected with his in tacit reminder of their chat before he turned to Amy. "You deserve a bit of fun, Tweety Bird."

Terri nodded. "Especially after Derek. What a prawn he was."

"We agreed never to mention him again." Amy placed her glass on the table and pushed her chair back. "I really don't feel like coffee. Would you mind if we called it a night?"

"Sweetie, I'm sorry. Please don't go because I mentioned that idiot's name." Terri rose and came around the table to stand beside Amy.

"No, it's not that. I'm just tired."

Dan finished his drink and stood as well. "Thanks for a lovely dinner, Terri. I should take Amy home. She's had a long day. Johnno, see you at work."

Terri and Johnno accompanied them to Dan's car and stood, arms around one another, and waved goodbye.

"Should I be jealous of Derek?" Dan broke the silence as he waited for the change of traffic light.

"No." Amy slipped her shoes off and tucked her feet up under her skirt.

"Is he still on the scene?"

"No. And can we leave his name out of the conversation from now on?"

"Okay. I only wondered—"

"We went out together, people expected us to marry, then we split up. He left Mt. Isa. Now I'm going out with you. End of story." She turned her head away.

The light changed to green and Dan accelerated smoothly across the intersection. If the relationship had been serious and this Derek had dumped Amy, it would explain why Johnno was so protective of her. And why her mother was happy to see her only daughter going out again.

He glanced over at Amy. Her arms hugged her knees and her head leaned into the seat. Fighting the urge to pull over and wrap his arms around her, he concentrated on driving. Amy would share the details or not, as she chose. But if ever he met the unfortunate Derek, he'd have to decide whether to thump him or thank him. On balance, both seemed appropriate.

"Here you are. Home again." Dan switched off the engine and waited.

Amy wasn't making any moves to get out of the car.

"Do you want to talk?" He touched her shoulder. "Amy?"

Incoherent mumbling and a slight readjustment of her head against the headrest looked suspiciously like she'd fallen asleep. Loathe to wake her, he turned the radio down low.

The veranda light came on. Jessie walked to the top of the steps and peered out towards his car. Dan chuckled. Amy's mother probably assumed they were saying goodnight as couples do.

He sighed and opened his door. Sitting in the car all night while Amy slept curled up on his seat might sound romantic, but would do neither of them any good. Carefully, he opened her door, undid her seatbelt and lifted her out. She snuggled into his neck but didn't stir as he carried her into her house.

"Is she okay?" Jessie always seemed to hover around her children. No wonder Amy felt she had no personal space.

"Exhausted. She fell asleep in the car on the way home from Terri and Johnno's place. If you show me where her bedroom is—"

Jessie gave him an odd look. "I thought you—never mind. Last on the right."

At the end of the hallway, he eased the door open with his foot and entered Amy's bedroom. A queen-sized bed stood in the centre of a large room with French doors opening onto the back veranda. Under other circumstances, he'd have been delirious to find himself in here with Amy. Alone. At night or anytime.

"I'll turn down the covers before you put her to bed." Bustling past him, Jessie pulled back the white waffle blanket to reveal pale blue sheets and turned on a funky, modern bedside lamp.

Dan set Amy down on her bed and eased off her sandals before pulling a sheet up to her waist. Streaks of golden hair caught the soft light from the lamp as she turned her head into her pillow. As much as he'd enjoy staying, watching her sleep, holding her, he hadn't been invited. Ever.

"I'd better be going then. Night, Jessie."

Jessie put a hand on his arm and smiled. Hazel eyes of a darker shade than her daughter's looked up at him. "Dan, you don't have to pretend with me."

"What do you mean?"

"Amy's a grown woman. That was really sweet of you, asking which was her room, but we're not old-fashioned. If you're used to staying the night here, please don't go on our account." Jessie turned and walked out, pulling the door closed behind her.

Which left him in a quandary.

To stay or not to stay? What a question. Expectation and his own desire warred with what he knew was right.

He ran his hand through his hair and headed for the door. Without Amy's invitation, it was wrong, regardless of her family's expectations. If Jessie was in the lounge, he's just tell her he had to be up early and didn't want to disturb Amy.

"Dan?" Amy's sleepy voice stopped him in his tracks.

He sat on the edge of the bed and tucked her hair behind her ears. God, she was lovely. "What's up, Sleeping Beauty?"

Struggling to keep her eyes open, she held his hand in both of hers. "You haven't kissed me goodnight."

"Are you saying you want me to kiss you? There's nobody here to see us." And he wouldn't take advantage of a sleepy woman. When he kissed Amy, he wanted her wide awake, knowing it was him, a flesh and blood man who desired her.

She tucked his hand beneath her cheek and looked at him. "Kiss me, Dan."

Her light floral perfume teased his senses, and she knew whose hand she held. Exulting in her subconscious desire for him, he kissed her forehead. Beneath his lips her skin was soft and warm.

Her hand slipped behind his head and she ran her fingers through his hair. Sleepy-eyed, her gaze connected with his before she tilted her head.

Dan defied any man to resist the petition of her sweet mouth. Softly, he kissed her lips, revelling in the closeness, resisting the urge to deepen it. Drawing his hand from beneath her cheek, he raised their joined hands and dropped a kiss into her palm before closing her fingers over it. For such a chaste kiss, he felt ridiculously happy.

"That's for sweet dreams. Goodnight, Amy." He turned off the lamp and tiptoed from her bedroom.

Chapter Twelve

Amy slipped her hand into Dan's as they walked through the backstage door into a hum of voices and bustle of activity. "I wonder how Terri's feeling about the first dress rehearsal?"

Dan gently squeezed her hand and linked their fingers as they skirted the props table. A couple of the boys from the workshop appeared carrying two painted palm tree cut outs. Dan drew her into a small space between a papier mâché rock and the wall, giving the boys room to manoeuvre the awkward shapes in the crowded area. Wedged into the tiny space, his cologne wafted around her, teasing her into inappropriate awareness of him. At times like this, she almost forgot their pretence. As Dan's knuckles brushed her thigh, darts of longing for more than he could give made her turn away before she forgot they were playing roles both on and off stage.

Beyond the black curtains they'd helped Terri hang last night as temporary wings, two loud thuds echoed followed by Terri's raised voice.

"Not there, upstage means the back of the stage, not the front. Do you think that stage plan shoved in your pocket is directions to dinner? Read the plan—please!"

"Sorry, boss." Dave's reply was cheeky, but respectful. The boys adored Terri and she'd had no trouble enlisting a workforce for the weekend set up.

"From the sound of that, I'd guess Terri is—stressed? Come on, we should get out there and help."

Amy took a deep breath and reminded herself they had work to do as she followed Dan. They edged around the papier mâché rock that took them in front of a painted scene of sea and beach.

Mike jumped out from behind the flat, yelling a challenge and striking a pose like a Maori warrior doing the haka.

Amy squealed and jumped back.

"Gotcha, Tweety Bird!" Mike grinned and strutted around, beating his bare chest like a giant gorilla.

Dan's hands gripped her shoulders and held her against his chest. His long, lean length plastered to her back set her heart thudding harder than Mike's prank. She raised a hand to her chest and leaned back. For a handful of moments, she committed to memory the feeling of his body against hers.

Dan released his hold and stepped back.

What was wrong with her? They were friends, not lovers. Her silly manoeuvre had probably made him uncomfortable.

A chorus of laughter rose behind them and Amy looked over Dan's shoulder. A group of women from the office and a couple of young apprentices stood in two groups. Dressed in plastic grass skirts and bikini tops, and boardies, they exuded energy and excitement and fun.

Terri appeared onstage behind Mike. "What's with the jungle noises from you lot?"

Mike leaned against the props table and whistled like he was completely innocent. "Hi, Terri."

Terri sighed. "I might have known you'd be at the centre of any hijinks, Michael Maguire. Now, make like the wind and blow on stage. Rehearsal begins in two minutes."

"Yes, memsahib."

"Amy, hi, I need you. And Mr Music, get your A into G—please."

Dan sat in solitary splendour behind his sound and lighting desk at the rear of the hall and adjusted the brightness of the side spotlight. Amy's skit was going surprisingly well for a first dress rehearsal. She'd used Mike's extrovert nature cleverly and given him the chance to shine.

It was an innate part of her nature to give everyone a chance, like she'd given him. Except when she threw herself completely into the role, she was likely to make him forget they were pretending.

Like when she'd jumped into his arms after Mike had jumped out and scared her. As he held her, and the sweet scent of Amy filled his nose, he'd all but forgotten they were surrounded by people. And when she pressed back in his arms, he had to ease away or risk her feeling how much he really wanted her.

"Hey, Dan?" Terri's voice cut through his reverie.

With a start, Dan realised the music had ended while he'd been lost in thoughts of Amy's backside pressed against his groin.

"Can you dim the spot? I want to talk through that last act before we run it again."

"Sure, Terri." He dimmed the lights and sat back, flexing his fingers and stretching his arms above his head.

A hand slid over his shoulder and a soft curvy chest pressed against his back.

Amy. He reached behind him and encountered a rounded bottom that gave him ideas of where he'd prefer to be right now. He squeezed lightly and turned his head.

A whiff of heavily spiced perfume reached him as a mouth—not Amy's soft lips—touched his neck. He jumped up and turned quickly, knocking his chair over with a crash that drew all eyes to him.

And Sharyn standing beside him with a feline smirk and bikini strap slipping down one shoulder.

"Dan, are you okay?" Amy hurried over, her gaze flicking between him and Sharyn.

"I'm fine. Sharyn got me like Mike got you earlier." Dan deliberately raised his voice. From the stage, a few people laughed.

Tess applauded and called out, "Goodone, Shazza."

Terri clapped her hands and recalled attention to her. "From now on, can we leave the practical jokes at the stage door? In seven days, we have a fully booked out fundraiser and one full dress rehearsal between now and then."

Murmurs of agreement floated among the ensemble as Sharyn climbed the side steps of the stage. As the cast turned their attention back to the director, Sharyn cast Dan a look that was pure sexual invitation.

Cold sweat ran down his spine and memories of Carissa and Gosford roared back. Anger and worry mixed together and bile rose in the back of his throat. It couldn't be happening again. Not here, not now he'd found Amy. Hands clenched on the desk, his lungs struggled to pull in enough air. Would Amy understand? Would she believe he hadn't initiated anything with Sharyn? How could she?

And then Amy was standing in front of him. She held his hands and turned him away from the stage. "Dan?"

As his vision cleared and he looked into her worried eyes, the band around his chest eased.

"I thought it was you behind me."

"Oh, and I made you fall out of your chair?"

"No, I mean I thought it was you at first. But you don't wear heavy perfume and then when I realised it wasn't you—"

"You tipped your chair over. Okay."

"Amy, I didn't encourage her. I swear I didn't even know she was there."

"I get it." Her thumbs stroked across the backs of his hands. "Terri looks like she needs you now."

He drew a deep breath and nodded.

Amy sat at the tiny stage manager's desk behind the bamboo screen and sorted out her rehearsal notes. She had a couple of cue changes for Dan when he finished packing up his sound system and a list for Terri. Several friends had stopped at the desk and invited her and Dan to join them for a drink when they finished. "We'll see how we go."

As another pair of footsteps strolled past beyond her line of sight, she readied a smile in case they stopped to wish her goodnight.

"I give it a month, max." Tess's whiny voice carried through the curtain.

"That's being generous. Two weeks, tops." Sharyn always had the last word.

Wondering who Sharyn had her claws out for this time, Amy's mouth snapped shut.

As the women's shoes clattered over the wooden floor towards the exit, Sharyn's voice carried back. "She couldn't hold Derek's interest, and she won't hold the doctor's for much longer. Not after tonight. He needs a real woman, not a trouser-wearing frigid female. The miracle is he even looked at her in the first place."

Their voices faded as the outer door closed behind them.

Chest tight, the edges of her vision blurred. Anger, long suppressed, surged through her.

Beside her, Dan dumped his armload and took her hands. He eased the pen from her grip and dropped it onto her clipboard before taking hold of her shoulders and drawing her to her feet. "Amy, look at me. Don't give her words more weight than they deserve."

"I don't give a snap for Sharyn. Or Derek. He wasn't the man I thought he was."

"Probably not. But—"

"Forget it, Dan. This was a stupid idea from the start." She pulled away from him and ran. Anywhere was better than facing Dan's sympathy and pity. Out in the car park, she looked around for her ute before remembering Dan had given her a lift.

The backstage door opened and banged shut followed by the sound of boots crunching over the gravel parking area. "Amy, why did you run away?"

"Just leave me alone. I'm going home." She strode towards the gate. The way she was feeling, the walk home might help to burn off some of her crazy frustration and anger.

Dan didn't know whether to be more angry with Sharyn or himself. How could he have embarked on this crazy scheme with Amy and not considered the consequences? There were always consequences and if he couldn't convince Amy to take a chance on him, she would be the one ridiculed.

He'd promised he wouldn't hurt her but being with him had put her in Sharyn's firing line.

He reversed out of the parking space and pulled out onto the street. A few metres ahead, Amy was striding out as though on a field march. He eased alongside her and lowered the windows.

"Amy, please get in the car."

"Go away."

"I'll take you home, or for a coffee, whatever you want, just get in the car."

"I don't want anything. Just leave me alone."

Ahead of them, the local park stretched for a block. Tall trees cast deep patches of shadow the streetlights didn't penetrate.

He pulled ahead a little way and got out of his car. Clicking the remote lock, he stepped out in front of Amy. She tried to side step and he moved to block her escape.

"Get out of my way, damn it." Her voice broke and she veered off into the playground. Stalking up to one of the picnic tables, she sat on the top and pulled her legs up onto the seat.

Dan sat beside her and waited. Gradually his eyes adjusted to the low light. He could just make out the line of her jaw and the white of her eyes. "Can we at least talk?"

"What's the point? It's not like we're a real couple."

"I know we started out pretending but—"

"But what? You can't change how things are. And you know what else? When you break up with me, I'll be stuck with that whole 'poor Tweety Bird, can't keep a decent relationship going more than a week' crap."

"Amy, I won't let that happen. I promise."

"Don't make promises you can't keep."

That was the problem. He couldn't control what Sharyn or anyone did. But he could damn well help Amy to deal with it. He'd got her into this and, no matter what it took, he'd make things better.

"You overheard something you weren't meant to and now you're just going to give up, and let a spiteful woman like Sharyn win?"

"What do you expect me to do? I won't stoop to her level and get into a slanging match."

"Of course not. But I want us to show her how wrong she is." Exactly how he'd do that he didn't have a clue. Yet. But no one was going to say those sorts of things to Amy and get away with it.

"And how do you propose we do that?"

"Leave it to me. Just promise to go with the flow, okay?" He reached for Amy's hand. At least she didn't pull out of his clasp. But she didn't lean into him as she had on other occasions.

"Why do I have a feeling I'm going to regret this?"

Chapter Thirteen

Combined with annual health checks, the clinic in the remote indigenous settlement had occupied most of the day. Dan swabbed the last child's arm then gave the five-year-old his injection.

"There you go, young fella. All done." Dan smiled at the boy and pressed a dinosaur Band-Aid over the speck of blood.

Luminous dark brown eyes peered up at him and the child shoved four fingers into his mouth before being scooped up by his young mother. She looked up shyly at Dan. "Thanks, doc. You good bloke. Tommy didn't like the other doc. He ran away and didn't get his needle last time."

"Well, he's up to date now, Elise." Dan took a green lollypop from the jar supplied by the RFDS for immunisation clinics and offered it to the child. "Would you like this, Tommy?"

The boy nodded and reached for the treat. He clutched it in his fist then buried his face in his mother's shoulder. As she reached the door, Tommy peeped over her shoulder and gave Dan a shy grin.

This was what his vocation was about, and the sense of rightness, of being where he was meant to be, settled over Dan. His grandfather had known the joy of service as a Flying Doctor back in the 1960s, and Dan's mother was still servicing a rural community in Central Queensland. Why had he settled for the Gosford job when rural medicine was in his DNA? Especially when that decision had cost him some of his integrity.

He pushed away the negative thought and focused on packing away his clinic. It was high time he got back to the joy of his job. Like Elise and young Tommy.

A light tap on the open door heralded Amy's arrival. "Hi, Dan. All finished?"

"Yep. This is the last box."

"Can I carry something for you? We need to get a move on." There was a definite edge to her voice, not annoyance but a thread of concern.

Dan paused in his packing and met her gaze. Definitely concern. "Did I run overtime? Sorry."

"No, but there's a thunderstorm moving in. I'll have to take the long way home and there's a chance we won't get around it." Amy picked up two medi-containers and headed for the door. "I've done my pre-flight checks. We'll take off as soon as you're on board."

Ten minutes later, Dan strapped himself in beside Amy. The view from the cockpit was stunning. And worrying. Thunderheads towered, a brilliant, glowing white barrier across the way home. Lightning flashed deep within the cloud mountains and bolts pulsed like heartbeats. Flickers of concern raced down Dan's spine and the hairs on the back of his neck stood on end. "Something wicked this way comes," he muttered.

"What was that?"

Amy didn't need the distraction of his rambling thoughts. "Shakespeare. Can I do anything?"

"No. I just need to get us out of here like thirty minutes ago." Amy radioed to base that they were taking off, having already lodged her altered flight plan. As she taxied to the end of the strip and turned for takeoff, she glanced across. "The storm has grown more quickly than I expected. This will be a rough trip."

Amy took off smoothly, considering the raw state of the remote runway. The Beechcraft climbed steadily to cruising altitude and she adjusted her course to the new flight plan. Through the side window, she kept an eye on the massive storm cell while monitoring the gauges and radio. Concentrating on her controls and the rapidly deteriorating weather updates left no time for chatting with Dan, who sat quietly, hands resting on his knees.

Miles from its usual route, off their starboard wing, a 747 was giving the storm a wide berth. The radio crackled as the commercial flight captain made contact. "RFD, Qantas 321, just advising poor weather ahead. It's closing fast. Suggest diverting to nearest secure landing. Repeat, storm closing fast behind us. You're heading into a ring of storms. Over."

"Qantas 321, RFD. Thanks for warning. We are turning back now. Over and out." Banking the plane in a slow, easy turn, Amy reset her co-ordinates before she contacted base and alerted them to the change of plan.

"Sorry, Dan, we're not going to get home tonight." Turbulence juddered the plane and they dropped suddenly in a pocket of air. Amy scanned the ground for emergency landing sites and hoped against hope it wouldn't come to that. Her hand slipped on the joystick and she wiped her fingers down her trouser-clad thigh. Would they make it back to the settlement before the wild storm caught up with their little plane?

"You'll get us home safely, Captain Just Amy. We're in good hands with you at the controls." Dan's voice was steady and his eyes and smile reflected his confidence in her.

She drew a steadying breath and eased her grip on the controls. "Yep. Gotta look after my passengers. So, best song titles for our situation, Doctor Dan?"

He thought of his study session the previous evening and grinned. "'Don't Bring Me Down'."

"ELO! How old is that one?" Amy snorted. "Are you sure you don't want me to land this bird? Or we could—you know—keep going 'On the Wings of an Eagle'."

"Old it may be, and yet, you know it."

The heavy beat of the song played in her mind against the background bass of distant thunder. "My parents used to listen to ELO. Got anything more recent than before I was born?"

"It was a top ten song in 1979 and, coincidentally, before I was born too. Still your turn."

"'Riders on the Storm', and it's your fault I'm back in the 70s."

"Top twenty in the US in 1971. How old did you say you were?"

"How do you know all those dates? Are you a secret trivia fanatic?"

"I used to play old 70s music when I was studying. It made the nights pass more quickly and I linked information with certain songs. A sort of mnemonic that got me through med. school." Dan hummed a couple of bars from The Doors' chorus then segued into the Bee Gees' 'Stayin' Alive'.

Dan's memory for music trivia was kind of endearing and geeky all rolled into one. Amy thanked her lucky stars he'd taken over from Dr Fraser who had never been a great passenger. The middle-aged doctor would have been clutching a spew bag by now.

"I Will Survive." Amy thought of her mum belting out that song at karaoke nights when they came into town. Pretending embarrassment, secretly she'd been proud of her mum's singing and confidence. Something she'd never have. Not in this lifetime.

"How about 'Stairway to Heaven'." Dan's offering coincided with several seconds of buffeting as the storm roared up behind them.

Descending further, Amy peered ahead into the dim western sky for a glimpse of the settlement. "That one's plain creepy at this moment. 'Summer Breeze', that's a nicer thought. Keep your eyes peeled, Doc. And see if you can raise Bill to turn on as many lights as they can for us."

"Will do." Calmly, Dan worked the radio but it was several tense minutes before Bill's voice responded to their call.

"We'll set flares out. Electricity supply is down and the generator's playing up." The elder's comment sank like a stone in Amy's stomach. Could anything else go wrong tonight?

Fully occupied with controlling the rocking plane, Amy wished her co-pilot hadn't picked today of all days to call in sick. Another pair of hands on the controls would have been welcome.

"Anything I can do, Amy?" At least Dan didn't sound like a passenger in panic mode. Calm seemed to surround him. Okay, maybe she was happy he occupied the co-pilot's seat.

"Can you see— there's the flares. Hang tight. This will be a bumpy landing." Amy lowered the flaps and eased back on her speed. With a thud and a bounce and a judder, she applied the brakes as the light flares rushed past in her peripheral vision. Finally, the plane stopped and she exhaled loudly.

"Always wanted to know what a joey felt in its mother's pouch as they bounced along." Dan touched her forearm.

She turned and met his gaze. "And now you do."

"Well done, Captain Just Amy."

A ridiculous prickling threatened her vision and she blinked several times. "All in a day's work, Doctor Dan. Come on, let's get this baby tied down."

Soaked to the skin, Dan raced back to join Amy as she struggled with the last tie-down strap. Wind and fat plops of rain had quickly become a torrential downpour, buffeting the plane and making their task more difficult. She tightened the rope and stood, staggering against his chest under the onslaught lashing them. Lightning split the darkness and he grabbed her hand, wrapping the other arm around her waist. Together they weaved a path towards the clinic, all but falling into reception as gusting wind ripped the door from Dan's wet hand.

He leaned his weight against the door and shut out the forces of nature. At the sudden cessation of rain lashing him from all angles, he exhaled and rested his forehead on the wood before turning to Amy. Above the roar of wind and thundering rain on the tin roof, he heard and saw nothing until white light stabbed a path through the impenetrable darkness and her hand reached past her phone flashlight. Cold fingers clasped his and she tugged him into the inner surgery.

Slamming the door, she slid down the wall and drew him down to sit beside her.

Shirt and trousers were plastered to his skin and water dripped down his face from his too-long hair but at least now they were sheltered. Rubbing a hand across his face, he leaned close so she could hear him. Sweet apple shampoo scented her hair and tickled his senses. "Are you okay?"

"I know I'm alive." And then she laughed. Not that he could hear her above the storm, but her phone torch revealed a Cheshire cat grin and her arm brushed across his.

A simple brush of skin on skin shouldn't have made him so—aware of her. But the chill of the storm vanished as his senses became ultra-tuned to her touch, and her scent, and the way her white shirt clung to her breasts.

Muscles tense, he eased away and created space between them. Maybe he should head back outside. At least the distraction of pelting rain might take his mind off the woman shivering next to him. Shivering?

Amy dropped her phone in her lap and rubbed her arms. Were her teeth chattering?

"Are you cold?"

"How c . . . c . . . could you tell?"

"Come closer—if you want to." He waited for her to choose, wanting and not wanting her to move nearer. All week she'd maintained her distance and several times, he'd caught Johnno watching him as he moved through the hangar. But he wouldn't push her. Amy needed space and time to put Sharyn's nastiness behind her.

His heart pounded as that night in Gosford tore through his memory. Carissa coming onto him in the pharmacy, pressing up against him. 'I so love working with you, Dan. Maybe we could—you know—get to know one another much better.' Wrapping her arms around his neck, rubbing against him. 'Dan, you want me, you know you'—her gaze flicking to the door and suddenly she was pushing him away—'let me go.' He'd been trying to free himself when her uncle walked in on them and all hell broke loose.

Struggling for breath as familiar tightness banded around his chest, his hands clenched. Not once but twice he'd been put in an invidious position.

Amy covered his hand with her cold one and squeezed. "That's a generous offer, Dan, all things considered. I wouldn't take you up on it if I didn't think I was going to shake every tooth loose." She shuffled across the wooden floor and leaned against his chest.

Backed into the corner but longing to hold her, he dropped an arm over her shoulders. Goosebumps disappeared as he rubbed a hand up and down her cool flesh. "Better?"

She nodded and sighed, the sound transmitted through her lips against his neck.

Touch, scent, the sound of voice as she joked about their situation, and the sight of her smiling mouth . . . Four senses sparked and fizzed. Suddenly, desperately, insanely, he longed for the fifth. One proper taste of her lips . . . And where would that leave them? Him? Desperate not to muck this up, he grabbed the last thing he remembered.

"What did you mean, 'all things considered'?"

"I know how hard this must be for you. I understand, truly."

"Because of Gosford?"

Beneath his fingers, her skin warmed with his rubbing while dread chill raced through him. She knew about Gosford. That wretched false allegation had been thrown out eventually and Carissa had been disciplined and transferred to a different hospital, but the stain on his integrity burned like a fresh, raw brand. Wherever he worked, the fact the falsehood had existed would make people wonder about him. Even Amy . . .

"You can't know how bad it can be. When everybody knows—"

"I'm sure no one knows. But if they did, they wouldn't care. At least, not now they're getting to know you. Do you really want to continue our pretence?" She lifted her head.

From her tone of voice, he expected to see pity in her gaze. Or Amy with her 'I'm trying to help' hat firmly in place. Either would be unbearable.

In the spill of light from her phone, she tipped her head back until their gazes connected. Hazel eyes darkened and a hint of the mints she sucked while she was flying teased his nose. There were no recriminations and pity was missing, thank God. But for some reason, she looked disappointed.

"Do you really believe they don't care? Mud sticks." He knew all about the surreptitious glances from mere acquaintances.

"Mud? I don't understand."

"Most people aren't so accepting."

"Honestly, Dan, that's Stone Age thinking. Nobody gives a damn if you prefer your own sex." Her eyelashes lowered, hiding her expression, and she pulled away.

In place of her lush body pressed against his, cold clarity washed through him. "What are you talking about? I meant—"

She thought he was gay? Like pieces of a jigsaw falling into place, her sometimes-odd behaviour around him made sense. Amy had been protecting him.

Dan didn't know whether to laugh or not at the absurdity of her deduction. He had mates and colleagues who proudly proclaimed gay pride and with whom he had marched and drank and shared a flat. And he'd brought his girlfriend du jour to their parties. He appreciated women, loved working with them. But Amy was different, special, and keeping her at a distance had been a new form of torment. And now this? Wanting her as he did, it was the ultimate irony.

"Amy, I'm not gay."

Chapter Fourteen

Amy shook her head, but her assumption about Dan couldn't be wrong.

Could it? Because if it was, that meant he didn't like her. Not like that. Period. Nothing more to say. She was the loser in the Relationships Stakes, just like her poor nag running last at the Cloncurry races. Why should that surprise her? Just one of the boys, she was. Good old Amy. Great to have around when your car broke down, or when you wanted a lasagne baked. But as real girlfriend material?

She sat back on her heels and eyed him like a bug on her windshield. "If you're not gay, why did you ask me to pretend to be your girlfriend? Why not ask someone more believable, like Lizzy?" Anger born of mixed emotions reared its head and she poked him in the chest. "What's wrong with me then?"

The air in the tiny surgery supercharged with more electricity than raged outside. Dan's nostrils flared and he took hold of her hand and held it against his chest. "Clearly we were talking about different things. My version of 'all things considered' isn't about you thinking I'm gay. It's about what happened before—"

Savagely he bit off the rest of his sentence and pushed to his feet. She swung around, aware her mouth hung open at his outburst. He took two strides and she saw no more as her phone toppled onto the floor and plunged the room into darkness.

"Amy, are you okay?"

Shuffling footsteps were followed by a thud, a swear word, and the sound of the metal desk scraping over wooden floorboards.

Groping for her phone, her fingers closed over a leather boot. As it slid along the floor she yelped. "Stand still. I'm right in front of you."

Dan's hand touched her hair but his feet stayed in the same place.

With her left hand she felt around, leaning out further and frantically patting the floor. On all fours, she touched the leather phone case just as Dan switched on his phone. The torch beam projected a monstrous shadow of her onto the wall and she swivelled around quickly to face him. He'd probably been treated to a blinder of a view of her rear end poking up in the air.

Dan rested his backside on the edge of the desk and placed his phone beside his hip, its beam pointing to the ceiling. As far away from her as the room allowed, she noted miserably. Her anger seeped away into the darkness. Leaning against the wall, she pulled her knees to her chest and wrapped her arms around her legs.

"Are you okay? I didn't step on your fingers, did I?"

"No." Meeting his gaze was out of the question. Embarrassment seemed to stalk their interactions out of the plane. Maybe she should just accept that was karma for chucking a wobbly at him the day they met.

"Amy?"

"I'm sorry I got the wrong end of the stick about you. Can we leave it at that?"

"How did you come to that conclusion? Just so I know for next time."

If the floor would open up and swallow her right about now, she'd not complain. Rain drumming on the tin roof eased into a softer rhythm. "When you refused my invitation and then Mike invited you to join us and you smiled at him and scowled at me—"

"I didn't scowl at you. I was guilty that I'd been caught out having a pub meal after knocking back your invite but I didn't scowl."

"You scowled. And then you were really standoffish with all the young women at work but chummy with the blokes and I thought— I was wrong. Get over it." She lowered her gaze.

"Amy, it's not what you're thinking."

"You used me to keep the man-eater at bay. I'm just one of the boys and—"

"Stop right there. You've got it completely wrong."

"How? Look at you, way over the far side of the room."

Frustration spiked and he gripped the edge of the desk. "So help me, Amy, just listen for once. I've wanted to get to know you since I first saw you but we started off on the wrong foot. And there was Gosford, looming over me like a pall of smog."

"I get that it was tough, but I told you I believed you. So why did you need to pretend to like me like—that?"

"You told me you just wanted to be friends." And look how well that turned out. He had hoped to build on the friendship she was prepared to offer and show her that he really cared. Love hadn't been on the cards but he'd fallen for Amy. Hard.

"I liked you but I thought you preferred men. And it shouldn't have hurt but it did."

He tipped his head and hope, like a tiny white butterfly, fluttered in his brain. "You liked me?"

"Yes, Dan, I like you. Present tense. And I accept that friendship is what you're offering me."

She liked him. Dan couldn't get past that one, wonderful, hope-inspiring statement. "Why do you think there can't be more than that?"

"From your kisses. You kissed me like—a friend."

"So did you."

"I thought—"

"Don't say it." He held up one hand. Amy's misapprehension was laughable, ironic when he thought of the nights he'd fallen asleep with dreams of her. "With the number of cold showers I've had since I met you, I can only be thankful I don't live in Antarctica."

Amy shook her head. "If you wanted something more than friendship, you wouldn't be on the other side of the room."

Shoulders hunched, she pulled her knees to her chest and wrapped her arms around her legs.

"If I sit beside you, I won't be wanting to talk, Amy."

That brought her head up and her gaze collided with his. "You won't?"

"No. Do you know how often I've imagined kissing you? Not a peck on the cheek but properly, so you know exactly how I really feel about you."

"You know, Doctor Dan, they call me Tweety Bird but it seems to me you're the one doing an awful lot of talking."

"We've played song titles and hunt the torch. Or was that a version of Blind Man's Bluff? What else is there to do in a storm?"

She kneeled up, her body leaning towards his. "Come over here and let's find out."

Dan slid down the wall beside her, his eyes darker than before.

"What do you want to do, Just Amy?" He brushed a strand of hair off her forehead and cupped her cheek.

Dan was right to be wary after what had happened to him. Complete trust would take time to grow and she could be patient. But she wanted to know what his kiss would be like now that he wasn't—they weren't—

"Kiss me, Dan. Show me exactly how you feel about me." She leaned towards him and brushed her lips over his.

With a groan, his mouth came down on hers.

##

Dan's arm prickled with pins and needles but he refused to move. Faint dawn light through the surgery window revealed the curve of Amy's cheek as she nestled against his chest, and her warm breath stirred the hairs on his chest.

They'd slept fitfully as the storm raged and fallen asleep around two o'clock when the wind had finally died down.

Amy stirred in his arms and her mouth brushed his bare skin. She tipped her head up and opened sleepy eyes. "Morning."

"Good morning. Sleep well?"

She sat up and rolled her head from side to side. "I had a wonderful dream."

He raised his eyebrows and flexed his fist as he pumped feeling back into his hand.

"Or maybe it wasn't." Blonde hair fell over her shoulders and caught in his morning stubble.

He stroked a hand over her hair. "Tell me about it and I'll tell you if it matches mine."

For answer, she leaned in and kissed him, a quick peck that left him unsatisfied and worried that maybe he had dreamed last night's kisses.

"I need a toothbrush and breakfast." With a shy smile, she jumped to her feet and crossed to the window. "Looks like the storm has passed. Come on, I want to check the plane."

"What about breakfast?"

"Bill or someone will feed us." She opened the clinic door and stepped out as the first rays of sun crested the horizon.

"Looks like a beautiful, clear day ahead. You realise tonight is the fundraiser?" He draped an arm over her shoulders and kissed her ear.

She turned her startled gaze on him. "Oh, help. Terri will be having kittens that we missed the dress rehearsal last night."

"At least we weren't AWOL. Base knows we came back here."

Elise appeared from the nearest house, with Tommy hanging onto her dress. She waved when she saw them. "Hoy, you two, come on over for a cuppa. We're firing up the stove. How do you like your eggs?"

Chapter Fifteen

As Dan pulled into Amy's driveway, she was standing in the doorway keeping an eye out for him. He rounded the back of his car and stopped dead. Backlit by her veranda light, she was wearing high heels and a strapless red dress that hugged her curves in a way that sent his temperature soaring. He stood there, vaguely aware his mouth hung open while his hands itched to shape her contours.

"Will I do?" A note of uncertainty lay beneath her question.

Pulling his brain into gear, he covered the metres that lay between them and took her hand. "You're stunning in that dress. I'll be fighting off every male in the place to get a dance with you."

"Hi Dan." Jessie popped her head around the screen door and stepped out. She took Amy's other hand and held it high and twirled her daughter under her arm. "We went shopping this afternoon, after I had a look through Amy's wardrobe. Trousers and shorts, almost nothing suitable for a special night out. My little girl is beautiful, isn't she?"

"I've got the prettiest girl as my date. Coming, Amy?"

"We'll follow in an hour or so. Got your tickets?" Jessie pulled the screen door open and waved them off.

"Got everything, Mum. See you there."

Dan held the door while Amy sat and swung her legs into the car. As he got in his side and closed the door, her perfume wafted across, light and subtle and so very Amy. "What's that perfume?"

"Daisy. It was a present from my parents last Christmas."

"Suits you."

"You look pretty swish yourself."

He pulled up at a red light and turned to her. "Amy, before we get there, I want to be sure we've cleared the air."

"You're not gay, yes, I know."

"Right. But we are going out, for real now. You are my girlfriend?"

Amy looked away through her side window and gripped her hands in her lap.

Dan's stomach took a dive. After last night, he'd hoped they had got past Amy's doubts. But she'd been quiet on the return flight, and when they got back to base, she'd rushed away, telling him she had to get home. "What's wrong?"

"I'm not sure about going public as a couple."

"Like we've been doing for the past few weeks, you mean?"

"That was different. That was pretend."

"It wasn't pretence for me."

She glanced up. Fear and yearning vied for top spot in her eyes before a tiny smile appeared. "Me, too. Sometimes. Look, maybe I'm a little gun-shy."

"Since Derek? I figured that, but you were happy for people to think we were a couple when you thought I was gay. What's changed?"

"It's real."

"It was before, even when the reasons were different."

He took her hand and raised it to his lips. "It will be fun if you don't over-think it. Just relax and you may find you enjoy being with me. Will you give us a go?"

Dan held his breath, waiting for her answer. The light changed to green and the car behind beeped impatiently. "Will you?"

"I'll try. That's the best I can promise, Dan."

"That's all I ask."

They drove the rest of the way in silence.

As they walked through the backstage area, friends welcomed them both but their gazes kept returning to Amy. Most of the men looked as though they were seeing her for the first time and Dan couldn't help the spark of male pride as he tucked her arm through his.

"The blokes have never looked at me like this before."

"Told you, you look stunning."

Terri raced over, bright plastic leis draped over one arm, and grabbed their hands. "You don't know how thankful I am to see both of you. Amy, my God, you're gorgeous."

"Thanks." Amy's smile grew wider and she smoothed her hands over her hips.

"We wouldn't let a little thing like a supercell storm get in the way of this shindig. Besides, I set up my sound system this afternoon."

Terri's sigh of relief reminded him what a huge effort the organisation had been. She draped a plastic lei over their shoulders. "I've got these for you to wear. All the cast and crew have the same colour so the wait staff knows to keep refreshments coming to you guys."

"I'll go and do a final sound check before the doors open to the public. Amy, come with me?" Dan twined his fingers with hers and headed for the side stage steps.

"Hey, Terri, can you come check Mike's costume. I don't know what he's done but—"

"Coming. See you two later." She rushed off with a vague wave in their direction.

"Okay, sound system check."

Dan's set up was cordoned off behind low partitions covered in black material. He reached under the table and pulled out a secure box of lapel microphones, each labelled with a number. Checking the code, he handed the tiny mike to Amy. "Put this on, then go on stage and talk to me. I want to check overall levels before I call the first group of performers."

"Where should I clip it?"

"On your dress near your mouth." He switched the power on and checked the pre-sets. Out of the corner of his eye, he saw her moving the mike from one side of her chest to the other. "What's the matter? Isn't the clip working?"

"Um, nowhere is near my mouth."

"Here, let me do it." He took the mike and raised his hand to attach the clip to her dress. But as he looked down, his mouth dried. Even in four-inch heels, Amy was petite and his gaze zeroed in straight down her cleavage. Each time she inhaled his hand brushed her breast. If his life depended on it, he couldn't move.

"See what I mean? I have nowhere to attach it."

"No—er—um—"

"Dan?"

He sat quickly and turned away. "Just—er—carry it in your hand and hold it collar-height."

"Okay."

As her heels clicked across the wooden floor to the stage, Dan gulped in a deep breath and adjusted his trousers. Amy was skittish enough without having to deal with the ribald jokes and innuendo that would come their way if he were seen in this state.

He cleared his throat and depressed the PA button. "Mr Music to Tweety Bird, what's the forecast for tonight?"

Standing centre stage, Amy was bathed in the bright spotlight. Her dress glowed jewel-red and diamantes sparkled on her strappy shoes. She'd never looked lovelier.

She raised the mike near her mouth. "Tweety Bird to Mr Music, looks like we're in for stormy weather. Do you want me to keep talking?"

"Yeah, I need to adjust a couple of levels. Recite something."

Mike sidled up beside her, slipped an arm around her waist, and grabbed the hand holding the mike. "Tweety Bird, I'm in love. Run away with me to Blue Hawaii and we'll swim and surf all day."

"You're a dag, Mike."

Laughter filtered through from the wings. Mike grinned and swept Amy into an impromptu dance around the stage. Her giggles were captured by the radio mike and, silly as it was, a shaft of jealousy raced through Dan. If only Amy was happy to be with him, openly and wholeheartedly. Shadows from her last experience still haunted her. 'Gun-shy' she'd labelled it. Ironic that it had taken a gun to make him see what he really wanted.

He leaned forward and depressed the PA button. "Got it, thanks, Mike. Amy, ask group one to come onstage for a mike test."

"Hey, doc, you're doing a Mike-mike test. Get it?"

Amy shook her head and left Mike holding the clip on device.

##

"Hey, Ames, your skit was great." Jeff gave her a pat on the back as the dessert plates were cleared from their table. His eyes looked brighter but there were still dark shadows beneath them. If the tossing and turning coming from his bedroom every night was any indication, his leg was more painful than he was letting on.

"Thanks, big bro. Shame you can't take a turn around the dance floor with me."

"Yeah, crutches kind of cramp my style. Maybe Dan will dance with you when he puts the auto play on."

Jessie leaned over and patted her arm. "Why don't you go and encourage him to join us now the show part of the evening is over, dear? I saw him heading out that side door a few minutes ago."

Amy had noticed Tess dragging Dan through one of the exits. Suspicious of feral females, Amy had decided to give him five minutes before she went backstage too. Only to rescue him, of course. She refused to allow that she was jealous of Tess's grasp on his arm because that would mean acknowledging how important Dan had become to her. Letting him get close would make her vulnerable again. She didn't want to give another male that power over her heart.

"I'll be back shortly." With an apologetic smile, she pushed her chair away from the table and smoothed down her dress.

Skirting tables, she slipped through a side exit from the hall and made her way to the wings. Most of the cast would be eating their dinners out front and there were still the final major items to auction off before the dancing began.

Behind the upstage curtain, two voices rose and fell in tones of question and answer. Male and female.

Dan.

His voice sounded like when he was with a patient in one of his clinics. Amy had heard him often enough to recognise the sound of his examining voice. Much to his amusement she'd mimicked him as they flew home. Maybe one of the cast had injured themselves. Tess had looked anxious as she pulled Dan out of the hall. Indecision and an unwillingness to intrude held Amy back.

So why didn't she turn around and go back to her table instead of tip-toeing closer? Unsteady on her high heels in the dim light, she put a hand out as she rounded the props table. One of the cast had left their mike on the table and she picked it up to return to Dan.

"You've got such a gentle touch, Dan." That voice. Softer than her usual strident tones when talking to Amy, Sharyn was in full seduction mode.

Amy's stomach clenched. Maybe it wasn't seduction Sharyn had in mind but a real relationship that Dan's pretend romance with Amy had stifled. What if Sharyn really cared for Dan? It would explain her recent odd behaviour.

Of course, if Amy cared for Dan like that, she'd do everything in her power to win him too. But she didn't care like that—she couldn't.

"I can't see anything wrong with your ankle. Perhaps you've pulled a muscle. Elevate it on a chair until you go home."

"I didn't want Tess to bother you but she insisted on fetching you. I was in such agony when I came offstage."

"No problem. It's better to check these things."

"So true." As the cat-that-got-the-cream voice purred on, Amy held her breath.

Sharyn hadn't shown any signs of being hurt in the last act, and Amy was sure the woman would have made a fuss if it meant being the centre of attention. Yet no one was around to see this performance.

"Can you help me, Dan? I need a pair of strong arms to hold me."

Amy's internal radar pinged long and loud. Forcing a calm she was far from feeling, she rounded the black curtain and stopped. Head lowered, Dan's back faced her. Sharyn's arms draped around his neck and she pressed against his body.

Seeing the woman in Dan's arms shouldn't have mattered. It wouldn't matter if Amy didn't care for him. But her heart knew otherwise. At the sight of Sharyn in his arms, it cracked wide open.

SUSANNE BELLAMY

Chapter Sixteen

Sharyn's arms pulled Dan's head down as she plastered herself to his front like a leech. He closed his eyes and raised his hands to free her grip from his neck. Behind him, a strangled cry was quickly cut off.

He grasped Sharyn's wrists and freed himself, and turned. Pale-faced, Amy clung to the curtain.

"Oh dear, Dan, I think Tweety Bird has caught us out." Sharyn's fingers dug into his forearm like claws.

"Amy, it's not what it looks like." He stepped towards her.

Without a word, she turned and ran.

Bile rose in his throat as the nightmare closed in around him. Sharyn's grip on his arm tightened as the stage door slammed. Stupid to have thought he could escape the ghosts of Gosford. Stupid to think there would be no repetitions. Amy had seen them at precisely the wrong moment and confirmed her worst fears. Derek had done a number on her and shaken her self-confidence and now—he'd done the same.

Gut instinct had warned him not to be alone with Sharyn and yet he'd let Mike take Tess away.

"Take your hands off me, Sharyn." Somehow he kept his voice neutral while his heart was yelling denial of his loss.

"Dan, don't be like that. I just made it easier for you to recognise we're made for each other. You and Amy didn't even behave like a real couple."

Amy opened the door into the hall and squeezed past people turning towards the empty stage.

Barely holding herself together, she kept moving. Only the pressing need for either money or her car keys so she could escape had drawn her inside.

"And how do 'real couples' behave?" Dan's voice came over the PA system. A thread of anger underpinned his coolly polite tone.

"Touching, kissing. You never kissed—" Sharyn's voice was more sulky than sultry with the amplification.

Amy froze in the middle of an audience who listened with rapt attention to the disembodied voices. She craned to see past bodies blocking her view of the stage. Heat raced up her cheeks, the only part of her still warm.

But how was Dan and Sharyn's conversation suddenly being transmitted into the hall? And her private business? Had he accidentally left a mike switched on? Aware of eyes tracking her movements, she pushed her way through the crowd to Dan's control space.

How embarrassing. How bloody typical of her luck. She'd kissed him properly all right. In the clinic last night, they'd steamed up the windows.

"Yes, we did." Dan's response echoed her thoughts.

"Not you, her. She never kissed you properly. You'd have been tired of her in a month."

"Your last poisonous pronouncement gave us two weeks."

Mike stood at Dan's sound system desk with a satisfied smirk on his face. Beside him, Tess stood within the circle of his arm, looking up at him as though he was the embodiment of her dreams.

"Turn off the mikes. Please, don't make it worse."

"No can do, Tweety Bird. Don't want to upset the doc by messing with his settings." Mike's helpless shrug was belied by the mischievous gleam in his eyes.

"But—"

"I'm sure you misunderstood me." Sharyn's voice continued, oblivious of the fact everyone in the hall could hear her.

"No. You misread the situation. Amy is the only woman for me. And I hope one day to convince her that I love her."

"I love her." Dan's voice broke through her trance. She gripped the edge of the desk and turned slowly towards the stage. Did he know Sharyn's radio mike was on?

The PA crackled to life with Mike's voice. "Paging Doctor Dan. Doctor Dan, you're needed in the main hall. Please come immediately."

Dan appeared onstage from the wings. What did he have left to lose? His heart felt as heavy as a stone in his chest. He raised a hand to shade his eyes and peered out over the crowd. "I can't see a thing from here. Who needs me?"

Above his head, the PA voice guided him. "Here, Doc. At your control centre."

Dan hurried down the stage steps. Smiles, grins, nudges, he noticed them without paying much attention to the rest of the world's happy state. His own heart might be breaking but someone needed his attention and he had to get his thoughts back into a professional state in order to deal with it.

A path opened up through the crowd and someone patted him on the back as he passed.

"Good on you, mate."

"She's a great girl, doc."

And then he was clear of the last table. Ahead of him, Amy stood in front of the black-covered desk, her dress a rich red beneath her pale face. He stopped in front of her, waiting to hear if she would listen to him, if he might have a chance to show her how much she meant to him. But first, he had to see to a patient. "Where's the emergency?"

Mike leaned over the desk and pointed at Amy. "Here, doc."

"Amy? Are you hurt?" It didn't make sense but he ran a professional gaze over her. Nothing jumped out at him, other than her beautiful hazel green eyes.

120

"Did you mean it?"

"Amy, bizarre as it sounds after what you saw, I swear Sharyn means nothing to me. Tess fetched me to look at her friend's ankle."

"I see."

"I think it was a set up by Sharyn."

From the security of Mike's arms, Tess piped up. "It was a set up, doc. I didn't know she meant to do anything. Honest."

"Okay." Amy wasn't giving away anything, but at least she was here, and she was listening to him.

"She claimed to need help standing and grabbed me. You arrived and saw—"

"Her in your arms."

"Oh, God, Amy, it's Gosford all over again. Only this time, I might lose the most precious thing of all."

"Dan, did you know Sharyn's radio mike was on?"

"No, it wasn't. I turned her off before Tess called me to help."

Mike leaned forward, and Dan finally processed the fact he was standing in front of the control console. "Sorry, doc, guess I accidentally turned her mike on. Heard every bitchy word she said."

"You heard—everything?"

"Everything." Tension radiated off Amy. "Why did you say— what you said?"

"I wanted to make it absolutely clear to Sharyn that my attention is firmly fixed elsewhere. On a blonde bombshell who flies through storms and out the other side and with whom I am madly, desperately in love. But I don't want to scare her away by telling her until she's had time to decide whether she wants to go public with me."

"Too late for that, Dan. You told the whole of Mt. Isa." Amy's gaze held his.

"So—what would you say?" He took her hand and ran his thumb across her knuckles.

She tightened her hold. "Tell me to my face this time."

"I don't care if everyone knows it. I love you, Amy."

"Then let's show them how it's done." Amy slipped into his arms and raised her face to his. Her lips were soft and sweet and there was a promise in her kiss that filled him with joy.

BOOK 2
HEARTBREAK HOMESTEAD

Chapter One

Lizzy Wilmot looked at the congregation assembled to farewell her brother. Despite growing up in separate households after Mum died, a twinge of sadness for Jeb and the man he might have been brought a lump to her throat. Few people remembered they were siblings since her adoption by Aunt Trish, and Lizzy hadn't expected so many of her friends and colleagues at his funeral.

Beside her, Donna, her sister-in-law rocked her two-month-old son and dabbed her eyes with a soggy tissue.

"I don't know why I'm still so teary after everything that happened but I can't seem to stop crying."

"He was your husband. No matter what Jeb did, it's tragic his mental health issues led him to take his life."

"It's not Jeb's fault. He couldn't— damn." Donna's tissue fell to pieces and she reached down for her handbag with one hand.

Lizzy held her arms out to take her nephew while Donna scrabbled for more tissues. At eight weeks of age, Daniel Campbell was the most beautiful baby she'd seen. And if she had anything to do with it, he'd grow up like his brave mother and avoid the abusive behaviour common to the Campbell men.

"You've got nothing to be sorry about, Donna. Jeb behaved appallingly to you. Don't forget, both you and Dan might have died if not for the Flying Doctor."

Fresh tears welled in Donna's eyes. "I've never seen Jeb lose it like he did when the doctor wanted to bring me into hospital. He really thought I was going to leave him."

Lizzy patted her shoulder. "If it's any comfort, I think he was sorry for what he did. He did let you go." Unlike their father who had refused to allow their mother to leave 'Craeborn'. They'd lost both their mother and baby brother. Lizzy had used that memory to convince Jeb to put away his gun and let his wife be taken to hospital.

'Don't be like our father. Trust the doctor and let us take Donna to hospital. Now.'

'Take her. Get out of here.' Jeb had turned on his heel and that had been the last time she'd seen him.

Donna gulped back a noisy sob. "Yes. He let me go. If you love someone . . ."

"See, deep down, he must have cared about you." Although Lizzy doubted any man could hit a woman he truly loved but the half-truth would provide a little comfort for Donna on this difficult day. As Donna dabbed at her eyes Lizzy frowned; Donna's face was gaunt and shadows filled the deep hollow beneath her eyes. And her frequent teary outbursts had encouraged Lizzy to seek counselling for her sister-in-law.

"He did. He loved me, and he would have loved Dan if he'd had the chance. He always said a child needs both parents and your father was better when your mother was still alive. I don't know what I'll do now. How will I bring Dan up without his father?" Donna slumped onto her shoulder, her tears soaking Lizzy's white blouse.

As she cradled her nephew, Lizzy mulled over why Donna grieved so much for a man who had mistreated her so badly.

Donna sat up and wiped her shaking hands over her cheeks. "The thought of anything happening to Dan scares me witless. I don't want to go back to the property."

"Too many bad memories. I know what you mean. I'll be happy if I never see that place again." Goose bumps traipsed down her spine. The memory of her brother aiming a gun on the doctor and pilot who had responded to Donna's radio call, while Donna lay screaming in childbirth invaded her sleep. How much worse would it be in the house where her father's rages had seeped into the very walls? If not for Dr. Dan Middleton, Lizzy doubted either Donna or young Dan would be here today. No wonder Donna had named her son for the Flying Doctor.

"Hey, Donna, how are you doing?" Amy Alistair, the RFDS pilot who had flown Donna to the hospital during her labour, kissed her cheek before turning to Lizzy. "How's young Dan? He's grown a lot."

"He sure has." Over Amy's shoulder, Lizzy spotted John Padstoke entering the chapel. "Hey, can you sit with Donna? There's someone I've got to see."

"Sure." Amy slid in beside Donna.

Handing Dan to Amy for a cuddle, Lizzy slipped along the side aisle towards the double glass doors.

"Mr. Padstoke?"

The stooped, grey-haired lawyer stepped out of the line of people coming into the chapel and joined her in the space between the glass door and a plaster column.

"I received a message you wanted to see me as soon as possible?" she said as he held her hand between both of his.

"My condolences on the loss of your brother, Ms. Wilmot. I didn't mean today. It's a difficult time for your family. Could you call into my office at your earliest convenience? Would two o'clock tomorrow afternoon suit?"

"I can be there. I assume this is to do with my brother's will. Does my sister-in-law need to come too?"

"Ah, perhaps it might be—easier if we discussed things without her."

He was right. The business of today was to bury her brother.

##

"Elizabeth Wilmot to see Mr. Padstoke." Lizzy smiled at the receptionist and turned to take a seat.

"Ms. Wilmot, please come straight through. He's expecting you."

She followed the trendily dressed thirty-something woman down a corridor and waited while she knocked on the end door. "Ms. Wilmot is here."

Lizzy stepped into the office and Mr. Padstoke came around his desk to shake her hand.

"Thank you for making the time to see me. I'm sure you have a lot to do but time constraints make it imperative we talk with you as soon as possible. May I introduce Alex Carter?"

Dressed in a dark grey suit and burgundy tie, Carter's white shirt contrasted with his olive skin. Dark brown eyes fringed by thick lashes widened as their gazes met and a spike of sexual chemistry punched through Lizzy's body with the force of a tsunami. His face was too angular to be conventionally handsome but an aura of power surrounded him.

Momentarily deprived of speech, Lizzy held out her hand. Despite the warmth of his skin as he shook hands, and the flare of sexual awareness in his eyes, there was something hard about him. His mouth was set in a tight line; beautiful but cold, it looked as if it had been chiselled by a sculptor.

A premonition of something not quite right sent a frisson of fear down her spine. Pulling her gaze from his lips, she squared her shoulders, and raised her chin. "How do you do, Mr. Carter?"

His eyes narrowed so fleetingly before his lips parted in a polite half smile, Lizzy wondered if she'd imagined the assessing look.

"Ms. Wilmot. It's a pleasure to meet you. I'm sorry for your loss." In contrast to the stony features, his voice was a rich baritone and it reached inside warming her like a Cognac on a cold night.

He waited until she was seated before taking the seat next to her.

"I thought this meeting was about my brother's will. How do you fit into the picture?"

"A straight talker. Good. What we have to discuss comes directly as a consequence of your brother's will. How much do you know about his business?"

"Nothing. We were not—close."

Mr. Padstoke drew a document from the yellow folder on his desk. "I have a copy of Jeb's will for you to take away and study at leisure. There are provisions in here for his widow and child. There is one section in particular that demands urgent attention. It's to do with the responsibilities attached to ownership of the family property."

"Didn't he leave it to his wife and child? 'Craeborn' has always passed to the eldest son." Why was the solicitor talking to her about inheritance? As emotional as Donna was, it would be hers to make decisions about for her son.

Mr. Padstoke took off his glasses and polished each lens. "Inheritance rights aren't written in stone. I suspect there is a great deal we don't know about Jeb but one thing is certain; he hated his wife's family and would do anything to ensure 'Craeborn' didn't fall into Tait hands."

"I don't understand. Donna is a Tait and he married her. How can you say he hated her family?"

The solicitor settled his glasses on his nose and picked up the will. "Perhaps your sister-in-law can shed light on that for you. What I can tell you is that Jebediah made provision for his wife and child, but 'Craeborn' does not form part of their inheritance."

Lizzy shook her head and a chill ran down her spine. "Then who inherits it?"

"You, my dear. 'Craeborn' passes to you."

You can find Heartbreak Homestead here:

amzn.to/1nqc9hc

More Books by Susanne Bellamy

Heartbreak Homestead (Hearts of the Outback Book 2)
amzn.to/1nqc9hc

Long Way Home- (Hearts of the Outback Book 3)
amzn.to/**28taN8Y**

Second Chance Love (Amazon Australia store) amzn.to/1FEJyx4

Second Chance Love (A Bindarra Creek Romance)
bit.ly/1O5ngaN

Second Chance Café – Four Short Stories by Susanne Bellamy,
Elizabeth Ellen Carter, Noelle Clark and Abbie Jackson
bit.ly/1QlViZl

Sunny with a Chance of Romance amzn.to/1Cmy9jM

One Night in Tuscany amzn.to/1dKLyX6

One Night in Sorrento amzn.to/1brE2Jp

Winning the Heiress' Heart (The Emerald Quest) amzn.to/1B9TVUJ

A Season To Remember: Four Short Stories For Christmas – a book by Susanne Bellamy, Elizabeth Ellen Carter, Noelle Clark and Eva Scott

bit.ly/1ynJsTZ

Engaging The Enemy amzn.to/1wrYGHQ

White Ginger amzn.to/MiDjVr

You can find Susanne at the following:

Facebook: https://www.facebook.com/susanne.bellamy.7
Twitter: https://twitter.com/SusanneBellamy
Website: http://www.susannebellamy.com/
Pinterest: http://www.pinterest.com/susannebellamy/

Goodreads:
https://www.goodreads.com/author/list/6869630.Susanne_Bell
amy

www.ingramcontent.com/pod-product-compliance
Lightning Source LLC
Chambersburg PA
CBHW030653110726
47901CB00002B/694